THE BOSS AND NURSE ALBRIGHT

BY
LYNNE MARSHALL

All the characters in this book have no existence outside the imagination of the author, and have no relation whatsoever to anyone bearing the same name or names. They are not even distantly inspired by any individual known or unknown to the author, and all the incidents are pure invention.

First published in Great Britain 2010
Large Print edition 2010
Harlequin Mills & Boon Limited,
Eton House, 18-24 Paradise Road,
Richmond, Surrey TW9 1SR

ISBN: 978 0 263 21110 8

Harlequin Mills & Boon policy is to use papers that are natural, renewable and recyclable products and made from wood grown in sustainable forests. The logging and manufacturing process conform to the legal environmental regulations of the country of origin.

Printed and bound in Great Britain
by CPI Antony Rowe, Chippenham, Wiltshire

Praise for
Lynne Marshall:

TEMPORARY DOCTOR, SURPRISE FATHER

'A touching, tender and engrossing Medical™ Romance, TEMPORARY DOCTOR, SURPRISE FATHER is a wonderful story which I devoured in a single sitting! Don't miss this talented storyteller's enchanting tale of second chances, devastating secrets and the redeeming power of love!'

—*CataRomance.com*

'Lynne Marshall's excellent writing skills lend excitement and credibility to this story… The tension between Jan and Beck is realistic, and keeps you reading to the very end. A very satisfactory end!'

—*The Pink Heart Society Reviews*

This book is dedicated to the smartest
woman I know, my wonderful daughter and
future Nurse Practitioner, Emily.
Your beauty shines through your eyes
and brightens every room you enter.

CHAPTER ONE

JASON looked up from his desk to find big blue eyes staring at him. He'd been sailing all weekend and by Sunday, with nothing else to do for the afternoon, he'd come into the clinic to catch up on patient labs and charts rather than face being alone at home. The pint-sized human stood in his office doorway, watching him, unblinking.

"Man," she said. She wore a jacket which had slipped from her shoulders, held in place solely by her arms through the sleeves as she pointed at him. A simple pull-on shirt that didn't quite cover her pudgy tummy, and patterned pants in varying shades matched the bright green jacket. Corkscrew light brown curls surrounded her chubby face.

"And who might you be?" he asked, fighting off a sinking feeling as the memory of his daughter flashed in his mind.

Long slender arms swooped in and scooped up the child, who looked to be no more than two or three. Hanna had been four.

"OK, pipsqueak, I told you to stay by Momma." She didn't talk to the child like some parents did with high whining sounds, as if they were the favorite family pet. Her voice had a mellow, husky tone, like an actress from a classic movie. "Oh! I didn't know anyone else was here," she said.

He shouldn't be here, but the ocean had turned from glassy smooth to choppy and restless, and though the sun always soothed his emptiness by heating the cold blood pulsing through his veins, nothing seemed to help today. So he'd decided to work.

"Thought I'd come in to play catch up before another crazy week of overbooking." He stood and held out his hand. "I'm Jason Rogers, the family practice GP of this group."

The young woman accepted his greeting. Her

hand was cool and slender like the rest of her. He liked how her height almost brought her eye-to-eye with him, and how she looked at him as steadily as her daughter had.

"And I'm Claire Albright, the new Nurse Practitioner," she said with her child slung easily across her hip. "I think I'm supposed to remedy some, if not most, of that overbooking." She smiled just enough to show bright straight teeth. "You weren't at the meeting when they hired me."

"No." He dropped her hand and scratched the back of his neck. "I leave all that business up to the others." Phil, Jon and René had kept him emotionally afloat the last four years. In return his ample wealth had supported the clinic through its growing pains. He didn't know where or what he'd be without his medical partners.

The woman had ash-colored blond hair with streaks, like streams of light weaved through it. She had a high forehead and soft brown brows that showcased her hazel eyes. There was strength to her nose and chin, which he liked. He looked away.

Though definitely attractive, her appearance

didn't matter. Beyond his medical practice and patients, nothing much mattered. At all.

"I'm moving in down the hall." She seemed at a loss for what else to say. He wasn't helping a bit by standing like an idiot with his usual blank stare. "I love this building," she said. Her eyes shone as she mentioned the three-story cream-colored Victorian house turned medical clinic. "I used to drive by, read the MidCoast Medical Group sign, and say, 'one day I'm going to work there', and now I do."

Her enthusiasm pained him. It smacked of idealism and hope—things he couldn't remember. Jason couldn't think of an appropriate response, and stared blankly.

He'd purchased the mansion several years back for his partners' business venture with his wife's encouragement. She'd loved the building, too. Back then, the optimism now glimmering in Ms. Albright's eyes had resided in his heart.

"And this is Gina." With a mild blush across her peach and olive-tinged skin, her smile widened, pressing dimples into her cheeks, and it almost felt contagious. But he'd given up smiling a long time ago.

The little one ducked her head into her mother's shoulder, no longer bold. She'd no doubt realized Jason was not someone she could trust with her clear eyes and easy smiles.

"Hello, Gina. And Ms. Albright, you should be a good fit for our practice." He recited the hollow words to keep up the façade of being human—at least half human—for the child's sake.

Having completed his duty with a begrudging greeting, Jason sat down, sending a direct message that their introductory chat had ended. There was nothing more he could say. Not looking the least bit flustered by his blunt move, Claire nodded. The child on her hip squirmed to get down. She obliged, but held the girl by her shoulders and marched her down the hall without another word.

So the medical group had finally hired a fifth practitioner. They didn't want to bring in another full-time doctor, but had decided an RNP would be a big help. Besides seeing the routine overflow patients, she'd be counseling the diabetics and high cholesterol clients on diet and exercise. Or so René had promised. She could also perform physicals on both adults and children, and routine PAP smears on the female clients. The others would think of more to keep her busy as time went on.

René had mentioned something about the new employee taking a more holistic approach to patient care, whatever that meant. As long as her medical advice didn't get too out there, what did it matter to him?

Jason did have one concern about adding a fifth group member, though—what was he supposed to do with his freed up time? The clinic was as much of an escape from life as it was a means to practice his profession. If he ever caught up with his backlog, he'd be faced with dealing with the world outside. He couldn't afford to let that happen.

"Not exactly the friendliest guy on the planet," Claire mumbled to Gina, closing the door to her new office two doors down from Dr. Rogers. Her daughter scampered across the room, not interested.

Though overall he was good-looking, with straight brown windswept hair and strong masculine features, there was a deadness in his steel-gray eyes as if he'd had the life sucked out of him. It unsettled her. His empty gaze had sent a chill down her spine.

Jason Rogers struck Claire as a wounded soul. A fit and sexy man wearing a drab gray polo shirt and windbreaker who looked very much alive, but in his core he seemed damaged and unable to connect.

"It takes one to know one, Dr. Rogers," she whispered. The thought of reading his obviously broken aura both intrigued and frightened her.

Her snap assessment of her new employer didn't matter. She'd joined this medical group for the opportunity to practice a more inclusive style of medicine, not to make friends. And after the doozy of a job her ex-husband had done on her, her lagging self-esteem needed a positive boost.

They'd married young, with plans to travel the world. Shortly after their first anniversary, she'd started experiencing strange symptoms, which interfered with their plans. He'd been unforgiving, and chastised her over the next couple of years for not being strong enough when she couldn't finish a hike or a long bike ride. When she'd taken to bed with unexplained aches and pains, he'd accused her of faking it, as if she were nothing but a hypochondriac. A year later she'd become pregnant and things between them seemed to look up, but everything changed for the worse when she was finally diagnosed.

That was all water under the bridge, as the saying went. She'd learned so much in her quest to make her life better. She credited alternative medicine for giving her life back to her, and she wanted to extend her knowledge to her future patients here at MidCoast Medical.

She'd vowed that the new job was about what

was best for the patient. The total patient. For all she cared, if Dr. Rogers wanted to weave a standoffish cocoon or hang upside down in his office and spit at people, it didn't matter. She wouldn't give him the power to matter to her—as long as he left her alone to do her job.

Gina ran to the window and pointed to the sparkling Pacific Ocean off in the distance. "Pwetty."

"Yes, it is." Claire studied the resplendent view as a warm rush of excitement rippled through her. The clinic was situated in the heart of downtown Santa Barbara, a few streets over from State Street, the main boulevard. She stepped closer to the window and saw the pier through the palm trees. She'd definitely moved up in the world since, as a Nurse Practitioner, she'd also completed a degree in holistic medicine.

This was her chance to prove that medicine was evolving away from the old cut and dried methods to a more symbiotic approach connecting traditional medicine with holistic and alternative care. She treated the whole person, not just the physical aspect, but also the emotional, social and spiritual being. She'd already gained the other doctors' trust, when she'd introduced them to the world of homeopathy during her interview. They thought she'd be a good fit for their practice.

Claire was living proof that alternative *and* traditional methods worked best for chronic illness. She couldn't remember the last time she'd had a relapse from her Lupus, and she'd managed to keep her daily aches and pains to a minimum. As long as she kept everything in balance. She glanced in the direction of her new colleague's office; something about Jason Rogers knocked her off kilter.

Gina tugged on her pant leg. "Hungwee."

Claire scanned the several boxes yet to be unpacked. She grinned at the greatest gift she'd ever known. "OK. Give me a second." Her daughter smiled up with innocent, trusting eyes. It was almost two o'clock, long past lunch time. They needed to eat. Maybe after, Gina would take a nap while Claire finished setting up her new office and attached exam room.

The Victorian mansion, complete with wrap-around porch, gorgeous bay window and princess tower was big enough to house a spacious waiting room in what used to be the sitting room, while the receptionist's office would have been the dining room, and there was still room enough for three doctors' offices plus exam rooms on the first floor. The kitchen, pantry and laundry rooms had been turned into the doctor and nurse lounge, and the nurses' downstairs supply and procedure room.

The second floor, where Claire's office was, had been left to Jason and his family practice until she'd barged in. One of the bedrooms had been turned into a small waiting room for his patients, and another had become the nurses' upstairs station plus another procedure room. The high ceilings with crown molding throughout gave a spacious feel, and the wainscoting made each room special. The third floor had been left for storage, or so René Munroe had said when taking Claire on her initial tour a week and a half ago. Jason's door had been closed that day, and René hadn't made an effort to tap on it or to say hello.

Claire needed to pinch herself to believe she'd been hired into such a prestigious and beautifully housed medical practice. But what would it be like working down the hall from the standoffish Jason Rogers?

"Hungwee!"

If only everyone on earth could communicate as directly as a two-and-a-half year old, life would be so much easier. "OK, pipsqueak, let's go."

Claire thought about Dr. Rogers, alone in his office, and how René hadn't included him in the clinic tour. She wanted to make a good first impression, and decided to give him another chance. She popped her head around the corner of his door. "We're going to the health food store up the street for some sandwiches. Can I bring you one?"

He barely glanced up. "Oh, I'm about done

here. I'll grab something on my way home. Thanks, anyway."

OK, she got the point. Rogers wanted to be left alone, which was exactly what she'd do from here on out.

Monday morning was a blur. Claire had to get up extra early to get Gina to childcare in order to make it to the welcome breakfast René Munroe had planned at the clinic. Her muscles ached from all of the lifting, packing and unpacking she'd done yesterday, and she needed to add extra wild yam to her daily herbal cocktail to help ease the pain. So far, so good.

She rushed up the front steps of the clinic on stiff legs, across the potted plant-covered porch, through the entryway, past the reception office and into the kitchen at 7:45 a.m. Philip Hanson, the pulmonary doctor of the group, greeted her with a glass of fresh squeezed orange juice and a bowl of granola with blueberries on top.

"Since you're our homeopathy guru," he said,

"I didn't want to get off on the wrong foot with sticky buns or anything overindulgent." Though in his mid-thirties, he'd retained a youthful quality, and his broad, accepting smile helped ease her first day jitters.

Jon Becker, the cardiologist, called out a greeting from a table set with china, flatware and a peach-colored cover. "Join us," he said, as if she'd been working with them for years.

She sat next to him and reached for the cinnamon, and sprinkled some over her bowl of granola. Besides stimulating her immune system, cinnamon helped maintain a healthy cholesterol level; she never went a day without some.

Dr Becker's salt and pepper, close-cropped hair gave him a scholarly air. On the initial tour of the clinic, René had mentioned that Dr. Becker was a long distance runner, and his wiry build and angular features proved her point.

"Good morning, Claire. You'll have to excuse me if I'm not exactly perky today," said René Munroe, the OB/GYN element of the practice. She was already seated across the table from

Claire, with a mug of coffee in her hands. "I delivered twins last night."

"Oh, how wonderful. Everything go OK?" Claire asked, spooning her first bite.

"The mother had planned on a natural birth, but after the first baby was born, the twin slipped into breech and I didn't want to risk it." She swept a thick lock of auburn hair behind her ear. "She had to go through eight hours of labor and childbirth with the first baby, only to wind up having a C-section after all that."

"Oh, the poor thing!" Claire assumed the babies were at the local hospital, since it was the only one in town.

Though she'd known they'd planned this first day meal together, she couldn't take her a.m. meds at home on an empty stomach, so she ate her second breakfast, not wanting to insult her new partners. They all seemed so welcoming and friendly, and she had a great feeling she'd love working here.

Philip handed her a bran muffin, still warm

from the oven. "I baked them myself," he said with a proud smile. She noticed a deep and attractive cleft in his chin. René had also informed Claire that Phil had been an award-winning surfer in his youth, and his dark tan and blond-tipped hair suggested he still enjoyed the sport.

She broke apart the muffin and let the steam rise. It smelled like pure comfort, and her mouth watered in anticipation of the first bite. If she read her tea leaves, she suspected she'd see weight gain in her future.

After taking a bite and savoring the fresh-baked flavor, she brushed some crumbs from her skirt. Today she'd worn power purple. A simple patterned wraparound dress with matching necklace and shoes to make a good first impression. She'd also worn her hair down, had even curled it for the big day. She'd been caught by Jason Rogers in crop length workout pants and matching jacket yesterday, with her hair pulled back into a low ponytail, and she'd been a bit embarrassed about her decision not to wear a stitch of make-up, when, by chance, she'd run into him. Today she'd outlined her eyes in liner and had even worn mascara and a touch of plum-colored eye-shadow.

She glanced around the room. The circa 1900-styled kitchen hadn't changed much at all except for an updated stainless steel refrigerator, and microwave with stove combo. She smiled, thinking how the newer appliances matched the original tin ceiling. As evidenced by the dish drainer on the counter, they hadn't installed an automatic dishwasher. She liked how they'd used a tablecloth and someone had put a small vase of fresh flowers at the center. Everything felt homey at the clinic and it seemed filled with goodwill.

Two of the nurses strolled in, followed by the receptionist, and Claire got introduced. She liked how there didn't seem to be an invisible barrier between the doctors and nurses. They all seemed to greet each other and interact casually as they filled their coffee cups and nibbled on muffins, as though one big happy work family.

Claire was thrilled to be a part of it.

One person was conspicuously missing, though. Jason Rogers was nowhere in sight, and no one but her seemed to make note of it.

After breakfast, Claire went upstairs to prepare for her first patients. Gaby, the receptionist, had booked all the last minute add-ons who were willing to see the newest addition to the clinic, with her. Rather than make the patients wait for an appointment with their assigned doctor on another day, as they used to, this default system gave the clientele a sense of easy access to medical care. Down the hall, she noticed Jason's door ajar, but didn't dare walk over to say hi. He'd made it clear he wasn't the sociable type, and being a quick study, Claire knew she wouldn't be able to change him.

She sat behind her sturdy oak desk, adjusted her hips into the comfy leather-bound chair, and marveled at how her life had changed. A year ago her husband, Charles, had divorced her, and immediately had taken up with another woman who'd wanted little to do with children. Charles couldn't accept that he'd married a woman with a chronic illness and after her diagnosis, as the months clicked by, he'd grown more and more distant. Other than occasional weekend visits, poor Gina had been left on the sidelines of her father's new marriage.

Charles had let Claire know, in no uncertain terms, that he couldn't put up with her having Lupus. She'd been the same woman he'd met, fell in love with, and married, with the addition of a new diagnosis, but he couldn't understand that. She'd become imperfect to him, and he couldn't accept it. He'd made her feel guilty for getting sick, and ugly, when he'd look at her with disdain when her Lupus rash flared.

He was a successful businessman who insisted on a healthy partner to join him on adventures and extensive travel, and the once-loving man had shut down and turned away. Just like that. As if it was all her fault.

The pre-nuptial agreement left Claire with nothing beyond modest alimony and monthly child support payments. She knew Charles would come through in an emergency, but refused to depend on him for anything else. His not accepting her chronic illness had shattered her trust in both love and men, and she'd vowed to move on with her life—alone.

She'd recently had a stretch of good health and, with the new job, good fortune. As far as she was concerned, her past was just that. Over. And, with time, she hoped to get over the emotional damage, too.

Claire stood and moved to the window. She lifted the sash to allow fresh air inside and, gazing across rooftops, trees, and eventually toward the huge blue sea, she couldn't help thinking that her luck had finally turned.

By early afternoon, Claire had seen a dozen patients and was getting into the routine of the clinic's patient flow. Twenty-minute appointments were generous compared with the hospital where she used to be affiliated, which allowed only half that.

She read her next patient's records on her

computer, and heard footsteps down the hall, then a looming shadow covered her desk and Jason appeared. His mouth was in a straight line, and his eyes squinted tensely. He looked perturbed, to put it mildly.

"A back rub? That's what you recommended to Ruth Crandall to add to her medical regimen?" he asked.

Claire had seen so many patients already, she had to stop and think who he'd referred to. *The woman battling depression.*

"Well, I noticed she'd had her antidepressant increased at her last visit and her general complaints were unchanged. I thought we'd try something different."

"A massage?" He lifted a brow and handed the phone message toward her.

Claire read. Mrs. Crandall had called to tell him, after her visit that morning, what a great idea it had been to add daily massages to her routine, and how much she'd enjoyed meeting the new Nurse Practitioner. Under usual circumstances, a message such as this would be considered high praise, worthy of a pat on the back or handshake for a job well done. Evidently Jason Rogers didn't see it that way. His irritated attitude put her on defensive.

"Daily massages are invaluable for depression," she said. "They help relieve the aches and pains, and increase the release of endorphins for a sense of heightened well-being. There is healing power with touch."

"Is that so?"

Claire stood. "It's a perfectly good alternative to increased drug therapy. Wouldn't you agree that it isn't all about 'find and fix' anymore in medicine?" She waited for a response, but he just stood there with a steely glare. "Sometimes medical professionals need to integrate all avenues of health care for best results."

"You may have a point, but I've never once considered a massage as health care." He paced toward her framed credentials hanging on the wall. "Next you'll be prescribing aromatherapy, I presume."

She made a sly smile, and he caught her.

"Maybe I will." Their eyes met for the briefest of moments, and paused. He'd obviously come to reprimand her, but nothing in this lingering gaze could prove it. He investigated her face and she felt suddenly self-conscious. She fought off the urge to pat her hair, wondered if her lipstick had smeared. "I've studied alternative medicine, and I believe there is much to be said for balancing the systems. After interviewing Mrs. Crandall, I identified her as a specific constitutional type who would benefit from massage." *And, speaking of constitutional types, you'd be classified as uptight!*

"She lost her husband last year," he said. "She's grieving and depressed. My job is to get her through this rough patch with the medicine available and a grief support group, not to send her to a spa to waste her money for a superficial beauty treatment." He leaned his knuckles on her desk and stared deeper into her eyes.

Claire refused to back away. "The power of touch is hugely beneficial for depression," she said, staring back. "Have you ever tried it?" His left eye twitched. "I didn't tell Mrs. Crandall to stop the medications you've prescribed."

Jason eased back, no longer on the attack. "This isn't how we practice medicine here, Ms. Albright."

"You told her to get exercise. What's the difference if I suggest massage? And the only complaint I see in this phone message—" she waved the message in the air "—is your interpretation of it. I'd say she was thoroughly happy about her visit today."

"That's not the point," he said.

He seemed a bit unsure and she couldn't help playing with him. "So one of our goals *isn't* to make our patients happier?"

He tossed her an exasperated glance. "Just do me a favor and consult me first, Ms. Albright."

She had the urge to say *Aye-aye, Cap'n* but noticed his glare had softened, and the tension around his eyes had disappeared. He really wasn't comfortable interacting with people. Or was it just with her? Wanting desperately to make amends for any hard feelings, Claire smiled. "OK. But would you do me a favor and call me Claire?"

He glanced at her one last time, nodded in a stiff business fashion, and left the room.

Claire sat down and tossed her pen on the desk. She hadn't given the woman a list of herbs to run out and buy, or asked her to ignore her medicine. She'd merely suggested that daily massage might help her through her depression. And the patient had been very receptive to the idea, enough to send a complimentary message about her add-on appointment to her regular doctor.

Why did Jason Rogers have to be such a wet rag about it?

She ran her hands through her hair and thought about the man who'd left her completely confused. She didn't know his history, but would bet her first pay check that something awful had happened to him. Maybe he was one of those people who felt entitled to happiness and things hadn't panned out, so he'd turned bitter. Whatever the reason, on a whim, she decided to go out of her way to be nice to him. Just to bug him.

When her first day at the clinic was over, Claire gathered her belongings, and prepared to leave. In the future, she'd be careful when counseling Dr. Rogers's patients. One nasty run-in with him was enough.

Her eyes got big with the thought. She hoped Jenny Whatley, the university student, didn't tell Dr. Rogers about what she'd suggested for her daily eyestrain headaches.

Not one second later, as she shut down her computer, Jason came barreling into her office.

Claire set her jaw and straightened her spine.

"What the hell is natrum muriaticum, and why did you suggest it to my patient?"

"You've been reading my patient progress notes, I see." She tamped down her brewing anger over the fact he'd been checking up on her, and walked around her desk. She dared to look into his eyes and received a cold dull stare as her reward. This was nothing like the more reasonable man from earlier today. "It is commonly known as table salt and salt tablets are best used for chronic ailments."

"Such as…"

"Such as daily headaches from eyestrain and tension. Jenny Whatley has been complaining to you about her headaches for over a year. She has all the classic traits of someone out of balance. Her complexion is pale and waxy. She looks emaciated and has cracks at the corners of her mouth. She's anxious, irritable and stressed out. And she gets throbbing headaches everyday at the exact same time."

"For which I have checked every possible condition and come up without a reason," he said.

Oh, the old take two aspirin and call me in the morning approach, I see. She couldn't help the snide thought. Jason Rogers seemed to draw the worst out of her. "But you haven't solved her problem."

"She has tension headaches. What does table salt have to do with any of that?" he said.

"It can regulate and balance the body fluids."

He gave her an incredulous look.

In defense, she glared back. "I made sure she doesn't have any counter indications for taking these tablets. Her labs checked out and so did the physical exam. We agreed she'd try them for a month. And she'll call immediately if there are any adverse reactions, which I went over thoroughly with her, and *which* I predict won't happen."

"You don't belong in this clinic. We are a reputable medical clinic, not some hocus-pocus guesswork group. If you want to prescribe table salt to patients, then set up a stand at your local health food store."

Stung by his insult, she crossed her arms. "I beg your pardon?"

"You heard me."

René appeared at the doorway. "Is there a problem?"

"She's a quack," he said.

"And he's a closed-minded medical robot!"

CHAPTER TWO

"HOLD on. Hold on." René stepped between Jason and Claire in the cramped office.

Claire couldn't believe her loss of control. His insult felt like a slap in the face and she'd retaliated without thinking. How had he gotten under her skin so easily?

"I don't think she's a good fit for our practice," Jason said.

Claire's heart sunk to her knees. She needed this job. Her ex-husband's nominal child support payments barely covered the cost of pre-school and child care. As it was, she could only afford to rent the maid's quarters in a seen-better-days mansion in Montecito. She needed to provide a life for the two of them. She had to make this job work.

"If I've stepped over the bounds, then I'm sorry," Claire said, scrambling to make things right.

Jason's glare softened. Had he heard the desperation in her voice?

"I'm sure we can work something out here," René said.

"I thought we hired a Nurse Practitioner. Now I've come to find out we've got our very own faith healer."

"I will not stand here and allow you to insult me like that!" Heat burned on her cheeks. She'd meant to keep quiet, but his words cut to her insecure core, and she needed to stick up for herself. No one would be allowed to walk all over her ever again.

"Then I suggest you leave," he said with a glacier-cold stare.

Don't back down. Even though my livelihood is at stake, he cannot be allowed to talk to me as if I don't matter!

"I deserve just as much respect as you do, Dr. Rogers."

"Hold on, you guys," René interjected, her

gaze jumping wildly from Jason and back to Claire. "We can work this out civilly."

Jason shoved his hands in his doctor's coat and punched his tongue into the side of his cheek. He glanced at her desk, and the framed picture of Gina. "Only because she has a daughter to support am I willing to let her stay."

Who the heck did this guy think he was? The Emperor? *Well, how kind of you, sir, and I shall be forever grateful. Not!* "There are three other doctors in this practice who agreed to hire me. If you want to kick me out, I suggest you take a vote." With fear quivering her insides, Claire worried she'd pushed things too far. She fought to cover up her apprehension by widening her stance and leaning slightly forward.

Jason also leaned closer, and his glare delved into her eyes.

Why did she feel transported back to grammar school and smack in the middle of a sand box dispute? Back when boys and girls didn't know how to show they liked someone so they pretended to hate them. And why, upon looking closer into his eyes, did Jason Rogers appear to be enjoying himself?

"Hold on!" René said. "We don't need to take a vote. We can work this out like adults."

Claire wasn't sure what had clicked in Jason's mind, but his puffed up chest deflated infinitesimally and he stepped back.

"Look," he said. "I know with the economy the way it is, no one wants to lose a job." He ran his hand through his hair. "I'd appreciate it if you'd leave my patients alone. That's all. You can pick up the overflow for René, Philip and Jon. If you agree to that, I'll call a truce."

Claire glanced at René, who wore an earnest expression, as if encouraging her to take the deal. Accepting his offer for a truce seemed like the sane thing to do. Anything seemed better than standing around arguing with the obstinate and unlikable Jason Rogers. On her first day at work, no less!

If he wanted her to leave his patients alone, she'd be glad to comply. And once she was given the chance to get solid results with the other doctors' clients, maybe he'd come around to trusting her with his patients. And, if he asked nicely, she'd reconsider screening them for him.

She offered her hand, and he took it. The angry electricity that had jumped between them only moments before was still there. His palm was hot. And calloused, which surprised her. He stared intently into her eyes, and she almost needed to take a step back…but refused. There was something in his gaze that she hadn't detected before and, coupled with holding his hand, it knocked her a bit off balance.

"Truce," she said.

He nodded, dropped her hand and stepped away. After a brief glance in René's direction, he said, "Sorry to drag you into this." Then he went back to his office.

René stepped inside Claire's office and closed the door. "He's never offensive like that," she whispered. "He's sullen and moody, but never like that. I swear."

Claire studied her open-toed shoes, trying her

best to figure out what had just happened. "I'm sorry. I am so sorry. I'm never like this, either. Please don't hold this against me."

"Not at all." René cupped Claire's arms. "We want you here. We're glad to have you. You've got to understand that Jason, well…" She hesitated, as if she didn't know how much to disclose about the man.

Who knew what his problem was? Perhaps he'd been through a rotten divorce like she had, and he held a grudge toward women the same way she did toward men. Maybe they had more in common than either would like to admit.

"Jason," René continued, brushing her hair behind her shoulder, "how should I put it…he leads a lonely life, and sometimes he forgets how to treat people. His patients love him, though, and he's an incredibly good doctor. Just give him time."

"It's apparent that he cares about his patients, I just wish he'd be a bit nicer to me. Hey, I'm a tough girl. I'll live with this set-up. You know how much I want this to work out."

"Good, because he essentially owns the building and practice."

Claire's throat dried up. Of all the people to pick a fight with. She needed to sit down. "I promise this will never happen again."

René nodded and offered a reassuring smile. "Now, did I hear right—this was about table salt?"

Jason paced his office, exhilarated. A sensation he hadn't experienced in a while. All because of an argument with Claire Albright? Albright—hah! She couldn't have a more appropriate surname. Whenever she entered a room it brightened. She didn't need to wear that becoming purple dress to make a lasting impression. All she had to do was smile. He remembered how taken aback he'd been when she'd smiled and introduced herself to him yesterday. He'd thought about her smile once or twice last night when he'd dined alone in his big and empty condo.

So why did he feel compelled to chew off her head? Because she dared to approach his only remaining thread to life, his sacred craft of medicine, differently. Table salt and massages—what a bunch of bunk. Just the thought of it rankled him all over again.

But there was something more to his reaction. She made him "feel" things. He'd stared into her eyes and felt his heartbeat pound in his neck when he'd argued with her. He'd been hot-tempered about what he'd said because it related to his patients and medical practice, the only thing left he cared about, and she'd thrown the passion right back in his face.

And she smelled like cinnamon, which did crazy things to his line of thinking. He dug his fingers into his hair.

Damn. The strangest notion overtook him. It made him pace.

After four years in limbo, he almost felt alive.

He came to a dead stop.

He'd soon put an end to that "feeling" business, by avoiding her at every turn.

The next morning, Claire entered her office before Jason had arrived. She needed to work up the courage to consult him about a plan to help the waiting room patients relax. They'd gotten off on the wrong foot, and here she was with another plan, but she couldn't back down. It had come to her in the middle of the night; something he'd said in a snide way about "next you'll start aromatherapy" must have planted the idea in her subconscious. He'd absolutely hate it, but if her trial run worked out in the upstairs waiting room, she planned to suggest they try aromatherapy in the larger downstairs waiting room, too.

If Jason owned the building, and he didn't like her or her ideas, he could get rid of her without consulting the other partners. Though she hoped and prayed he wasn't anywhere near as big an ogre as she'd imagined.

Mid-morning Claire saw Jason escort an older woman past her office door. His arm was on her shoulder, and he wore a concerned expression. "Mrs. Lewis, I'm sending you to the best surgeon in Santa Barbara. We caught the lump early…"

This from the grumpiest guy she'd ever met? Maybe he wasn't so bad after all, and perhaps now was the perfect time to approach him.

She stood at her desk and waited for him to return. Her aromatherapy blend of lavender and ylang-ylang had been on the warmer all morning.

She used her hands to push the scent out her door, then rolled her eyes. This really was nuts—the markings of a desperate woman. The two things she needed to do to make him happy were to stay out of his way, and take care of every patient to the best of her abilities. But helping his outlook along with a little relaxing aromatherapy couldn't hurt, could it? Without his knowing, she might successfully change his sour mood and lift his spirits under the guise of helping their patients. And if it didn't work, no harm would be done.

She heard footsteps coming up the stairs and scrambled to her desk.

Jason slowed and hesitated outside her door. He turned his head and mumbled, "Morning."

Better late than never. Her mouth almost dropped open. Was he trying to be friendly?

"Good morning!" she said.

"What's that smell?" he asked.

Here was her chance. She popped up from her desk chair. "I was going to wait for you to get settled in and then tell…I mean ask you about this idea I got after we had our…uh…discussion yesterday. I mean last night. It came to me last night. The idea…I mean…"

"You're babbling, Claire. Get on with it."

OK, so he wasn't trying to be friendly, and she *was* babbling. At least he'd called her Claire.

"You've heard of white coat syndrome, right?"

"Of course." In his favor, he didn't look impatient.

"I was thinking about helping our patients relax while they're in the waiting room before their appointments by using a couple of essential oils that are known to calm people down. Would that be OK with you?"

He gave her the most curious look, as if she might be from an alien planet, but to her surprise he nodded his approval, then walked to his door and shut it soundly. She could have sworn she heard him mumble, "Whatever."

Claire ran behind on her morning appointments, and finished entering her last progress notes into the computer at quarter to one. She hustled down the stairs and into the kitchen to find it empty, except for Jason Rogers heating something in the microwave. She almost turned around and headed out the door, but he lifted his head, glanced at her and nodded.

Jason used a tissue to wipe his nose while he waited for his lunch to warm. "I needed to get out of my office. My eyes have been bothering me all morning, and now my nose is stuffed up."

The lavender and ylang-ylang? Claire widened her eyes, but caught herself from reacting too obviously. "Spring is just around the corner. Are you allergic to pollens?"

"Not that I know of." The microwave dinged and he reached for his lunch.

OK, so they proved they could have a semi-civil conversation.

Great idea, Albright. Instead of making him relax with aromatherapy, you gave him a headache and a stuffed-up nose. Maybe she should add some rosemary drops to the mix to help with decongestion.

She left the kitchen and ran up the stairs to turn off the aromatherapy diffuser in the waiting room. Maybe she'd overdone it, but none of her patients had complained. In fact, a couple of them had lower than usual blood pressures during their appointments that morning. She'd definitely add the rosemary drops tomorrow. Maybe his reaction had nothing to do with the aromatherapy.

She returned to the kitchen just as Jason was exiting. He glanced briefly at her when he passed, but didn't say another word. Could he have thought she was avoiding him when she'd run out of the room so quickly? And, just when they'd made a mini step toward progress, too. She wanted to throw up her hands. Instead of easing the tension between them, she'd succeeded in irritating his nose and giving him the impression she couldn't stand being in the same room with him.

Things were not going well.

Two of the nurses had arrived back from picking up takeout food, and sat chatting happily at the table. She nodded to them and pointed to the back door.

"It's so lovely out today. I think I'll eat in the garden."

One of the nice extras about having a Victorian mansion as a medical building was the well kept back yard and garden, complete with arbor, gazing globe, and fairy statues. English and painted daisies, camellias, bleeding hearts and crocus in pinks, whites and purples, and many other perennial spring flowers she didn't have a clue about, were so pleasing to her eyes in the garden, she couldn't resist eating outdoors. And though it was sunny and warm today, and she needed to avoid the sun because of her Lupus, the yard provided a huge ash tree for shade and a convenient bench beneath it.

She sat and inhaled to help her relax. Maybe she should have set up the ylang-ylang and lavender for herself. She rolled her shoulders and watched a couple of robins hopping around the verdant grass in search of food as she unwound. High in the tree, other birds called their greetings to one another and rustled the leaves as they flapped away into the sky.

This was the place she needed to be at this exact moment in her life. In this garden. At this medical clinic. She'd do anything she could to keep her job, even if it meant putting up with Jason Rogers. She took a bite of her grilled veggies and hummus sandwich and chewed contentedly…until…she noticed the bee.

Back in his office, Jason needed to consult his drug formulary and went to his bookcase to retrieve it. From his upstairs window he noticed Claire on the bench in the garden eating her lunch.

She'd worn a sunflower-yellow dress today, and had taken off her lab coat before she'd taken her lunch break. And she'd worn her hair down again.

He liked how it settled on her shoulders in waves. For someone who took herself so seriously, she certainly dressed in fanciful colors. Purple yesterday, bright yellow today. It said something about her, he didn't have a clue what, yet he found it curiously appealing and he felt drawn to her lively spirit. That disturbed him, made the hair on his neck stand on end.

He glanced at the picture of Jessica and Hanna on his bookcase that he kept out of view of others. Mother and child posed perfectly for the camera on one of their many vacations…so many years ago. God, he missed them. Was he being unfaithful to Jessica's memory by feeling a distant attraction to this new woman?

It wasn't purely about Claire being a good-looking woman, or the fact that it had been ages since he'd been intimate with anyone. No. And he definitely wasn't looking for anyone to become involved with. But Claire had guts and had stood up to him when he'd used his bully pulpit yesterday to call her out for trying new treatments. He respected her for standing up for what she believed in, no matter how off the mark she'd been. Table salt. Hah.

But really, what harm could a massage do to a depressed person? Had it been necessary for him to take such offense? First and foremost in the Hippocratic Oath he'd taken when he'd become a doctor was—Do No Harm. And Mrs. Crandall had sounded so hopeful in her message.

What did he know about hope anymore?

He shook his head, replaced the photograph on the shelf, and watched Claire as she bit into her sandwich.

Suddenly, she sprung up and her sandwich went flying as she jogged around in a circle flailing her arms. She flung her head around and frantically used her hands to brush her hair away. Over and over. With a contorted face, she danced in spasms and bent over, shaking her head, and swiped through her hair as if it were on fire. Again and again.

At first he was alarmed that something was terribly wrong. He started for the door, hesitated, then glanced back out the window. She wasn't calling for help. As she continued to gyrate and swat at the air, her fitful dance became…entertaining. Had something flown into her hair? If she gave one sign of being injured, he'd be down the stairs quicker than a three-star alarm. Until then, he'd watch from his prime position.

She stopped just as suddenly as she'd started. She smoothed the skirt of her dress and patted down her hair, then glanced around, as if to check if anyone had seen her.

A smile stretched across Jason's face as he observed a new side of Claire. A humbled, slightly embarrassed side.

Next he heard an unfamiliar noise. The sound of laughter. *His* laughter rumbling all the way up from his gut. It sounded like a foreign language, and he almost looked over his shoulder to see if someone else was making it.

After he turned his back, as he replayed in his mind Claire freaking out and jumping around swatting at her hair, he continued to laugh, a solid belly laugh. Why had the incident struck him so funny? Because it was so out of character for the woman. He really shouldn't be laughing at someone getting caught in a compromising situation. That was unkind, he thought as he wiped away tears from laughing so hard. She could have gotten stung by a bee and that would have hurt like hell. Though she'd shown no evidence of that. No, he shouldn't laugh.

Definitely no laughing.

He turned around again. She sat back down on the bench and ate the other half of her sandwich, after she'd retrieved the first half and tossed it in the trash. She glanced around a second time, no doubt hoping no one had seen her antics. She was obviously unharmed, except for maybe her pride.

And the replay of her dance in his mind made him laugh again. "Your secret's safe with me."

A few minutes later, he sat back at his desk, still grinning.

How odd it felt.

The next morning, Jason stopped at Claire's office door with an impish look on his face. It made her pause. He cleared his throat.

"I brought you something," he said. He reached into the sack he carried and withdrew a safari hat complete with a veil made of netting and handed it to her.

"What's this?" She stared at the object she'd only ever seen in the movies before.

"In case you decide to eat outside today," he said, one side of his mouth ticking into a smile.

The blush started at her neck and promptly rose up her cheeks. "You saw me?"

He nodded and grinned, a bright flash in his eyes.

"The whole thing?"

"As a physician, I needed to make sure you weren't injured or anything."

She covered her eyes and grimaced. "I'm so embarrassed."

"Don't be." He looked uncomfortable, his teasing stance having vanished as quickly as it had appeared. "Please." They shared a gaze, and she instinctively knew he'd meant no harm. "I've botched things up, I see." He scratched the side of his mouth. "I guess I'm out of practice."

"No," she said, lifting the hat even as her cheeks heated to what she assumed to be bright red. "This is very funny. Really."

On an awkward note, he tipped his head and went to his office.

Claire had to give him credit for trying to act like a regular person instead of a recluse. In fact it touched her. She collapsed into her chair and continued blushing for a few more moments, but decided her embarrassment was worth it to see Jason Rogers's gorgeous smile.

And, to remind her he had a sense of humor, she hung the beekeeper's hat on the antique coat rack in the corner of her office.

The next day, to her surprise, Jason personally escorted one of his patients to her New Diabetic Class.

"This is Leona Willis," he said, assisting the middle-aged lady to sit. "I think she can use a refresher course on diabetic care."

This was a change. Jason had specifically told Claire to keep away from his patients, and here he was delivering one to her. She smiled at the new student, and then at Jason, and felt a mild blush dance across her cheeks, which seemed far too much like it was becoming a routine. He seemed to hesitate before walking backwards to the door with an odd expression in his eyes. It made her pause to remember what she'd been talking about. "Where were we?" she asked the class.

"The importance of eating several small meals a day," one craggy old gent replied.

Claire nodded and, instead of concentrating on the subject, took one brief moment to ponder the fact that Jason seemed to be reaching out to her as one professional to another. The thought buoyed her spirit and set the tone for the rest of her day.

One week of truce with Jason had made working at the MidCoast Medical Center so much more bearable for Claire, yet she was still antsy about her first administrative board meeting. Jason couldn't have chosen a worse night. Monday was the one night this week her childcare provider couldn't keep Gina past six p.m. And the meeting was scheduled for six-thirty.

René had arranged for dinner to be delivered, but Claire brought a special kiddie meal for Gina at the local organic market. She tried to set it up as a "treat", telling her how she'd get to have her very own picnic while the grown-ups had their meeting. Gina didn't seem too impressed. Running a bit late, Claire gritted her teeth and pushed through the clinic's kitchen door with her daughter toddling beside her.

The others, Phil, Jon, René and Jason, were already seated and passing around their individual reports.

"I'm so sorry to have to bring Gina tonight." She glanced around the room for sympathy and understanding and found it with everyone except Jason, who'd made a merely tolerable glance her way. "Babysitter problems," she said.

Claire situated Gina in the corner with a few books and small toys, then opened and served her dinner after washing the child's hands with disposable wipes. "Be a good girl for Mommy, OK?" She tried not to plead but, depending on Gina's mood, her personality could range from introspective to gregarious, and there was usually no warning which way the wind would blow.

As the meeting went on, Claire got a glimpse at how the clinic ran through spending reports from Jason, trends in ailments from Jon, recommendations on being more efficient from René, and meeting the Occupational Health and Safety standards for clinic care from Phil. Just as Claire prepared to give her report, Gina decided she'd had enough self-entertainment.

She brought her favorite book and plopped it on the table next to Claire. "Read me," she said.

"Mommy can't right now. I have to work."

Instead of fretting, Gina picked up the book and went back to her assigned corner.

Claire took a deep breath and prayed she'd stay there.

"OK," Claire said. "René asked me to talk a bit about CAM–complementary/alternative medicine—and its prevalence of use amongst our client population. My statistics show that thirty to forty percent of the general population is using or has used some form of herbal compound in the past year."

Gina stood and opened her book. "Thnow White and the theven dorfs," she recited aloud to the wall.

René and Phil tried not to snicker.

Claire swallowed and continued. "I feel it is very important to identify which of our patients are using these herbal medications. Many patients think of them as dietary supplements or natural health products, not medicine."

"Onth upon a time," Gina recited as she paced back and forth in a similar fashion as her mother, pretending to read from the page. "A printhess had to run away from her meanie tep-mommy." She turned the page with great flair.

"Gina, honey, can you wait until later to read your book out loud?"

"Can she read already?" Jon asked.

Not wanting to pop Gina's bubble, Claire shook her head surreptitiously and mouthed no. "She's working on it," she said, with sing-song optimism for Gina to hear. "Wait until later, OK, honey?"

The child turned to the wall and continued to "read" the story in a whisper.

Phil grinned, and René mouthed "aw". Claire nervously glanced at Jason and, instead of finding a scowl, she noticed one corner of his mouth edged up into an almost-grin.

"I'm so sorry," she repeated to everyone.

"Not a problem," Jon said. "Continue with your report."

She raised her voice and rushed through her carefully planned presentation, hoping her daughter wouldn't make any more disruptions. Claire had run down the list of herbal compounds most frequently used, and had offered her theory why patients failed to report the medication to their care providers, when Gina grew louder.

"Who is the faw-wist of them all!"

Even Jason snorted a laugh this time. He stood, and Claire figured she'd never get her chance to propose her clinic-wide survey. But, instead of suggesting the meeting be adjourned, he walked over to Gina and crouched beside her. Claire blinked, thinking she was imagining things.

"Hey, squirt, I'll make you a deal," he said. "I'll read that book to you if you'll sit quietly for just a few more minutes. What do you say?"

Amazingly, Gina didn't cower or get embarrassed, as she so easily did with her father when he reprimanded her. "'Kay."

Jason nodded, stood and went back to his seat. Gina followed him, something he obviously hadn't planned on. Surprise widened his eyes when she brought the book to the table and crawled up into his lap. Without saying a word, he helped her get settled and, when Gina was sufficiently at ease, he nodded to Claire to continue as if a minor miracle hadn't just occurred.

Claire cleared her throat and said, "I would like to conduct a clinic-wide survey of our patients to find out who is taking which herbs. If you'll look at the handout, you'll see I've named the ten most widely used herbal supplements and identified the potential drug interactions, some of which can be life-threatening. I believe it is imperative that we know *every* pill our patients are taking."

The group of doctors seemed impressed with Claire's suggestions, and began a lively discussion of how to go about surveying their entire patient population. Claire noticed that Jason lightly stroked Gina's curls as he read each handout.

The man had never looked more natural. Or relaxed.

His unconscious gesture did wonders for Gina, too. The child had fallen asleep.

Fifteen minutes later, the meeting came to an end. After gathering all the reports and putting them into her briefcase, Claire glanced at Jason.

She caught him studying Gina's slack mouth with a melancholy gaze. It made her chest squeeze.

He was a father. She knew it. But where was his family?

She leaned over to retrieve her daughter. "Thank you," she mouthed.

"No problem," he said with a muted voice. But the torn look on his face contradicted his words. Somehow she knew holding her daughter hadn't been easy for him, and she instinctively knew she owed him a huge favor.

When Claire picked up Gina, she automatically woke up. "Man read," she said, rubbing her eyes and kicking her feet. *Oh, not now. Please don't throw a fit, child.*

Claire glanced at Jason, who had a soft but distant look in his eyes.

"I did make her a promise," he said, lifting the storybook.

Relieved, Claire delivered Gina back to his lap and the child settled in immediately, ready for her story. As though he'd read a million children's books, Jason began. "Once upon a time..."

As Jason read to Gina, Claire helped René gather up the take-out cartons and wash the flatware. She caught René's marveling glance, then nodded in agreement when she mouthed "wow". She kept busy, collected Gina's toys and books and carried everything to her car. She was on her way back into the clinic when Jason met her halfway down the walk. He carried Gina down the steps and hoisted her into her car seat expertly.

"Thank you so much, Dr. Rogers," Claire said.

"Call me Jason, will you?"

A look passed between them that said so much more than "truce". For the first time since she'd been working in the new job, Claire felt she belonged. And Jason had shown the first signs of crawling out of his cave.

Jason watched Claire and Gina drive off. The wrenching pain in his chest made it hard to breathe. He'd paid a price for holding that child.

Memories of cuddling Hanna had been dredged up from their carefully fortified cave: the softness of her hair, the perfection of her complexion.

He couldn't go on like this.

He clenched his jaw and watched the taillights turn the corner. He wanted to hit something. To take a sledgehammer and bash to smithereens the tomb that kept his daughter and wife from him.

That woman and her child had gotten under his skin, had forced him to feel things—things he never wanted to experience again. Feelings he couldn't bear.

The damp night air enveloped him as he bit his lip and paced against the torment.

CHAPTER THREE

TUESDAY morning, Claire passed the mock-up version of the patient herbal survey to Phil Hanson as he sat in his office. She'd stayed up past midnight putting it together. Aside from his medical school and specialty certificates framed on the walls, there were several surfing trophies and photographs of him with his board. His laid back attitude often carried over into his clothes, and today he wore a Hawaiian patterned tie with a pale blue denim shirt.

"Looks good," he said. His thick wavy hair appeared to only have been finger combed, yet he still managed to pull off a charming air. She wondered why he wasn't married, then remembered René had commented he was a happy and confirmed bachelor.

"What looks good?" Jason's deep voice came from over her shoulder.

It almost made her jump. She turned and found she was the closest she'd ever been to him, but the doorframe kept her from stepping back. His face was freshly shaven and he smelled of sandalwood and citrus, which tickled her senses. Though his hair was neatly trimmed, the longer top part had fallen across his forehead. She fought the urge to sweep it aside. Up close, his gray eyes had tiny flecks of blue in them, and they looked kinder than she'd thought. Or maybe that was because she'd seen him in a new light last night. After he'd read to Gina, her daughter had talked about him the entire ride home, until she'd fallen asleep.

"Well?" Jason said.

"Oh. The herbal survey. Here's a copy for your approval," she said, handing the pages to him.

He avoided her gaze, studying the paper

instead. In contrast to Phil, his stiff collared white shirt hugged his tanned neck, and he'd made a perfect knot with his drab tie. Someone needed to brighten this guy's wardrobe up, but it wouldn't be her.

After her disastrous marriage, she wanted nothing to do with men. In her time of greatest need, she'd been kicked to the curb by her husband. Hadn't the wedding vows said "In sickness and in health"?

"Looks good to me, too." Jason handed the survey back and continued down the hall and up the stairs. His dark gray, perfectly tailored silk suit molded well to his broad shoulders and narrow waist.

Phil cleared his throat. Claire snapped back to the task at hand, and retrieved the survey from the doctor. He had a funny look in his eyes, as if he'd caught Claire ogling Dr. Rogers, which may have been the case but she hadn't meant to be so obvious. Her cheeks heated up and she made a quick getaway.

In a room of men, most women would notice

Phil Hanson first, with his striking good looks and surfer boy features. But Dr. Rogers had a subtle solid handsomeness that caused her eyes to linger. After swearing off the entire gender, she wondered why she was suddenly comparing the men she worked with.

Claire shook her head, and strode to the receptionist's desk for the list of patient addresses.

"We'll need eight thousand surveys to go out," Gaby, the receptionist, said.

"Wow, this is a bigger practice than I thought." Drs. Munroe and Becker had already approved the survey. Now she had Phil and Jason's blessing, too, so it was just a matter of mailing it.

"That's the number of families, not the entire patient population. Some will need multiple surveys in one envelope."

"Oh, and do we have a budget to include a stamped return envelope?"

"I'll have to run that by Dr. Rogers," Gaby said.

Claire wanted this survey to be a success and knew that including the return postage made for a higher return rate, but she didn't want to break her employer's budget in the process. She mentally kicked herself for not getting the budget approved at the meeting last night.

"No problem. Dr. Rogers is a kitten. He'll do whatever I ask," Gaby, the plump, nearly fifty matron said, revealing yet another side of Jason Claire hadn't counted on.

She thanked Gaby, and felt relieved she wouldn't have to confront Jason a second time that morning, since he seemed to be pushing buttons she'd forgotten she had over the last year.

The concept of finding Jason Rogers attractive seemed ridiculous!

So why was she still thinking about him in his classy tailored suit?

Three days later, the first of the patient surveys were ready to get mailed. Claire sat with a stack on her desk, double checking to make sure no one had been overlooked. She glanced up to find Jason, looking tall and dashing, in her doorway.

History had proven that it was never good when Jason stood at her door. Her throat went dry before she could utter a sound.

He scratched the back of his neck. “I have a question for you,” he said.

On a rush of relief, she smiled.

He entered and sat in the chair across from her desk and leaned forward, elbows resting on his knees. “First off, I wanted to let you know that Jenny Whatley has told me she no longer has daily headaches.”

“That’s wonderful.” She’d already heard from Jenny but, being a lady, she hadn’t rubbed his nose in it.

With a conciliatory gaze, he continued. “I guess I owe you an apology.”

“Not necessary,” she said, though shocked that he’d mentioned her success.

He nodded, looking relieved. “So now she says she needs something for her anxiety, but doesn’t want to take any of the mild sedatives I’ve offered.” He stared into her eyes, and she found it hard to think of one single thing. He looked earnest and she realized he was having a difficult time saying what he'd come to her office for.

"Are you asking me to recommend an alternative medicine for one of your patients?" This time, she couldn't stop herself from rubbing it in, just a teeny bit.

He grimaced. "Actually, *she* asked me to ask you."

She grinned. "Ah. OK, well, I'd recommend valerian. As long as she's not on any other sedatives."

"No. None at all."

She told him the dose and what to watch out for, went to her bookcase and retrieved her favorite herbal medicine book. "Here. You might like to read up on it."

He nodded. "Thank you." And he looked sincere, which touched her in a gratifying way.

It was Claire's turn to hesitate. As if he could read her body language, he lingered in her office. She scratched her cheek. "You made quite an impression on my daughter the other night."

He gave a self-deprecating laugh. "She's too young and innocent to know the real me, I guess."

Claire reached into her desk and pulled out a crayon stick figure picture. "She asked me to give this to 'Man' this morning."

Surprise colored Jason's usual pewter eyes to a softer gray tone. "She still remembers me?"

"Talks about you every day. I tried to teach her your name, but…"

He glanced at the mostly-scribbled picture. "This is sweet. She's adorable, by the way."

"Thanks. I think so, too." And, since he seemed receptive to the latest drawing, she reached back into the same drawer and pulled out several more pictures. "She's asked me to give you a picture every single day since you read her that bedtime story Monday night." She handed them to him.

"You've been holding out on me?" His attempt at humor was gratefully accepted.

He glanced into her eyes and she could see pain written in his gaze. With anyone else, she wouldn't have thought twice about bestowing them with her daughter's latest artwork. But with Jason she wondered if she was being kind by sharing them, or causing him trauma.

He nodded, almost smiled, took the pile of papers and, without another word, left her office.

Over the next few days Jason enjoyed the respectful routine he and Claire had slipped into. If she arrived in her office first, he'd pause by her door on his way down the hall. He'd nod and say "Morning."

And she'd beam back in whatever brightly colored blouse or dress she'd chosen for the day. Dangly earrings waving, hair up or down, eyes flashing with life. No matter what the weather, her office seemed filled with light. And it always smelled good, too.

Cinnamon came to mind.

And if he'd beaten her in to work, she'd take the extra few steps to his door to say hi and wish him a good day. The added effort validated him as part of the human race, something he'd forgotten he belonged to.

He wouldn't admit to anyone, almost couldn't admit it to himself, but he looked forward to his daily greeting from Claire. The seeds of life seemed firmly planted in her being and, even though he'd grown used to hiding in the shadows rather than attempting to live like everyone else, he felt drawn to her brand of energy. Wanted to feed from it. And some days, since she'd come to the practice, he even felt like smiling.

Later that morning when Jimmy Dixon cried when Jason entered the examination room, and wailed after he'd made several attempts to look down the boy's throat, he decided to get backup.

"Excuse me a minute," he said to the distressed mother, then padded down the hall to Claire's office. She wasn't there.

He walked to her exam room and tapped on the door. She opened it just wide enough to peek out. She was gowned and gloved, and most likely in the middle of a pelvic examination.

"Sorry. When you're done could you help me out in exam room one?"

Her naturally arched brows lifted in surprise. "Sure. I'll be there in a couple of minutes."

Five minutes later she joined him in his office. Feeling a bit chagrined, he explained his predicament.

"I'm usually really good with kids, but Jimmy hates me, has since the first vaccination. His mother thinks he has strep throat, and I can't get him to let me touch him, let alone get a throat swab."

Claire smiled at his request, and he could have sworn the room got brighter.

"Sounds like me trying to get Gina to take liquid antibiotics," she said. "I'll give it my best shot."

"I'd better wait here." He sat in his office and thumbed through a pile of reports that needed his attention, but thought about the newest employee instead. Aside from her crazy attitude about alternative medicine being the answer to everything, she was undoubtedly pleasant to work with. He sniffed the air for the telltale sign of her fruity floral scent and enjoyed the added touch of cinnamon he'd always noticed around her. The woman smelled good, and he liked it.

Without warning, the image of his wife came to mind, and how she'd always smelled sweet like vanilla. He tortured himself with memories of how he'd loved to kiss her neck and inhale her scent. How she'd always caressed him back. He'd loved her so much, but feared her image was growing harder and harder to capture. He closed his eyes tighter to bring her back into focus, and massaged the sharp pain in his neck as the ethereal vision of his wife dissolved into nothingness.

"All done."

His eyes popped open. Claire stood in the doorway with the throat culture in hand. He didn't remember hearing so much as a peep from the examination room.

"How d'you do it?" he asked, still rubbing his neck.

"I have my ways," she said with a teasing glimmer in her eyes.

How could he be thinking of his deceased wife one second, and then be taken aback by the simplest gaze from Claire the next?

"Thank you," he said. His nurse walked by and took the culture from Claire on her way to the exam room.

"Anytime," Claire said, with the same glint in her eyes. What had gotten into her? "Maybe you should have that looked at," she said.

He screwed up his face, then realized she'd referred to his hand kneading his tight neck and shoulder. "Oh, it's nothing."

"If you change your mind, I'm also trained in acupressure." She wiggled her fingers in the air. "I could work that knot out in no time."

The thought of Claire touching him set his nerves on end. He covered by acting gruff. "I'll keep that in mind, Albright. Now, don't you have a patient waiting?"

She nodded, then mocked him with a salute. "Yes, sir."

He felt unnerved by the reaction she'd caused. He suddenly recalled the long-lost game of flirting with the opposite sex, and went completely still. A wave of unfaithfulness stopped him in his tracks, and the pile of lab reports received his undivided attention. Claire disappeared from his door without another word.

The next morning, Jason tapped on Claire's door wearing a perplexed expression.

"What's up?" she asked, noticing he was wearing a pale blue shirt under his doctor's coat that brightened his eyes.

"I have a patient who has red welts all over her back. She's trying to explain something to me, but I can't understand her."

This piqued Claire's interest. She rose from her chair and followed Jason down the hall. As they walked, he explained that the patient was a newly immigrated Chinese woman who usually brought her daughter along to interpret.

When they entered the room, Claire noted that the patient had a temperature, and she seemed congested and coughed into her hand from time to time. Claire introduced herself, but didn't offer her hand until she'd donned a glove.

"I was about to listen to Mrs. Ching's lungs when I noticed the welts," he said.

"I'm going to have a look at your back," Claire said to the patient, noticing puffiness around her eyes before stepping behind the exam table and opening the patient gown. When she saw the uniformly placed, fifty-cent sized welts across her entire back, she knew the answer. She closed the gown, removed her gloves, and motioned for Jason to follow her outside.

"She's been treated by a Chinese traditionalist and had a cupping."

Jason screwed up his face. "A what?"

"You've heard of Ying and Yang."

He nodded, his expression unchanged, which almost made her laugh.

"Her Yang is working overtime, and by cupping they tried to put her back in balance. The heat from the cups is supposed to suck out the toxins and restore her health."

"Well, it obviously hasn't worked this time around," he said. "She's feverish and congested and probably needs an antibiotic."

Claire nodded. "So her daughter made the appointment with you."

"I wonder if Mrs. Ching's daughter even knows she's been treated with Chinese traditional medicine?" he said.

"Good question. Why don't you give her a call?"

As Claire prepared to leave, Jason stopped her by reaching for her arm. The contact startled her, but she held her reaction close. "I would have put this poor woman through a full panel of blood tests to try and figure out what had caused those welts, if you hadn't been so astute. Your quirky background is proving to be very helpful."

A smile tickled across her lips, and Jason telling her that he appreciated her alternative medical expertise kept the smile spreading wider and wider.

"Cost-effective, even," he added, with a look of chagrin.

She opened her eyes with a mocking "no kidding" stare.

He shook his head and forced a partial smile. "And yes, that was hard for me to say."

She liked how his stately features seemed to pool into a puddle of warmth when he smiled. How his eyes relaxed and creases bracketed his mouth. Satisfaction trickled across her skin. "Then your compliment means all the more," she said.

He clicked back into his tough guy act. "Don't let it go to your head, Albright." She knew it was all show.

She gave him one last grin. "I wouldn't dream of it," she said, and turned to leave.

The third week after Claire Albright's arrival, Mrs. Crandall had responded beautifully to daily massage to the point of having her anti-depressant decreased. Jenny Whatley continued to sing the praises of table salt, the waiting room patients commented how much they enjoyed the pleasant aroma while they waited for their appointments—the very same aromatherapy which no longer sent him searching for a tissue. Jason had changed his mind about Claire's alternative voodoo practices.

After reading her *Herbal Medicine* book from cover to cover, he decided to test her out and refer one of his patients to her.

"*Forty-nine-year-old Hispanic female with chief complaint of ongoing hot flashes. Hormone replacement is not an option. See patient history. Seeks alternative phytotherapeutics.*"

Proud that he'd even used her terminology, he signed his name and marched down the hall to hand deliver the request for consultation. He wanted to see her reaction. Wanted to see her brighten and smile the way he'd come to enjoy. And he was fully prepared to receive an I-told-you-so smile—and even looked forward to it!

Claire's door was closed. He tapped, but no one answered.

He thoroughly trusted his office staff, and

assumed she'd requested a day off that he didn't know about. Why should he? Her personal life was none of his business.

Jason walked back to his office and checked the schedule. Claire was supposed to be at work today.

Before he saw his next patient, he trotted down the stairs and asked Gaby where Ms. Albright was.

"She called in sick, Dr. Rogers."

He tilted his head and went back to work but, before he reached his office, he slid his consult request into her in-box.

The next day, her door was still closed and the consult was exactly where he'd left it. And on the fourth day, Thursday, he marched into René's office.

"Jason, this is a surprise."

"I was wondering where Claire has been, and if she's all right."

René's greeting smile faded. "She's had a setback."

He sat. "What do you mean?"

"I think she has some sort of chronic ailment, and she got a virus which has knocked her for a loop."

"Has anyone checked on her? Is she all right? What about the child?"

"I'll call her later, if you'd like."

Thinking he'd like to be the one to call her, he deferred to René's offer. He had no business checking up on Claire. She was merely a business associate. Would he run out and call Jon if he was home sick? Why treat Claire any differently?

On Friday, René came to Jason's office. "I wanted to let you know that I've spoken to Claire. She is still quite miserable, poor thing. But she's hanging in. Maybe she'll get her strength back over the weekend."

"Yes. Well, I guess flu can really take its toll." He didn't want to let on to René how worried he was about Claire and her daughter. He had no right to be.

Then he remembered that Claire hadn't signed up for automatic deposit and today was a pay day. The other day, when she'd wiggled her fingers in the air at his office door, he'd noticed she didn't wear a wedding band. And by the way little Gina ate up his attention when he'd read to her, he suspected there was no man in her life. Someone needed to make sure she got paid.

Gaby had left for the day. They closed the clinic down two hours early every other week on Friday afternoons.

As soon as René left, he looked up Claire's home address and made plans to deliver her check. He could postpone his planned weekend sailing trip until Saturday morning.

Jason chastised himself for allowing "feelings" to inch back into his life. He had no business getting "involved" with anyone. He was emotionally DOA—what could he possibly offer another living soul? He pictured Claire's natural beauty and her disturbingly alluring personality, and shook his head.

She'd been off sick all week, she needed to get paid, and…maybe she needed a doctor?

* * *

The Italianate-styled house in Montecito suffered from years of neglect. Thick ivy vines covered the entire façade with cutouts for windows and the huge front door. The mansion sat in the middle of a cul-de-sac in a secluded neighborhood on a hill.

Jason parked his car and got out with the warm package he'd brought. He inhaled a faint hint of smoke. The last wildfires had come dangerously close to this area, and evidence of charred trees and hillside were in abundance in the near distance.

He strode under the portico to the door, and used the heavy brass knocker several times. After what seemed like close to a minute, a faint voice on the other side asked, "What do you want?"

It wasn't Claire. In fact the voice seemed ancient and quivery.

"I'm here to see Claire Albright. She works at my clinic."

The door squeaked open, and a frightfully thin woman with opaque skin marked with a map of blue and pink veins looked curiously into his face.

She was dressed neatly, in clothes like his grandmother had used to wear. A wool skirt, with a sweater set and supportive black oxfords. Her mostly-white hair was pulled back into a thin knot.

"I have her home address as yours. I wanted to deliver her pay check. I'm sorry if I've made a mistake."

He could see the woman weighing the circumstances in her mind. He was a stranger. Claire was a single mom. Yet he knew he looked official.

Jason reached in his suit pocket and held the pay check in a neatly addressed envelope for the woman to examine. If she didn't trust him, she could deliver it to her tenant, though admittedly he'd be disappointed. He flashed a smile. The kind he used to gain the confidence of his patients.

"No mistake. Claire and Gina live in what used to be the maid's chambers. And, since she works with you, I guess it would be all right. There's a separate entrance at the back of the house." She stepped outside, and pointed him around the corner of the gravel-filled driveway toward the back yard.

The first signs of twilight were bearing down on the day. The path looked dreary and cold, but at the end a tiny bungalow had a large planter bearing a burst of color beside the entrance. He'd never imagined Claire living in such a place. Her rent payments most likely helped the landlady pay her property taxes in the upscale county.

His soles crunched on the gravel as a rush of misgivings slowed his step. What the hell was he doing here? He hugged the warm container. Right. Delivering money and holistic penicillin.

He reached the stoop, took the stairs two at a time, and tapped on the door.

After he knocked again, Claire's weak voice almost matched Mrs. Densmore's in tone.

"It's Jason. I've brought your pay check and, since I heard you've been sick, chicken soup to cure whatever ails you." He tried to sound light and jovial, nothing like himself.

She opened the door. "Jason?"

He raised his brows. "In the flesh. You gonna invite me in, or are you quarantined?" He worked to disguise the shock he felt at her pallor, her frailty, her droopy hair. Every last sparkle had left her eyes.

"I look a mess," she said.

"Hey, I'm a doctor. I deal with sick people every day."

She wore an azure-blue spa-styled robe, which seemed to gobble her up due to obvious weight loss. Her shoulders slumped and the furry slippers she wore made a shuffling sound across the entryway as she walked him inside.

A small, untidy living room revealed she'd been lying on the sofa, with a dented pillow on one end and a crumpled blanket cast over the back. The bright peach living room walls contrasted with the dreary hostess, and a fireplace served to keep her warm.

"So here's your pay check. Figured you might need it."

"How thoughtful of you."

"If you need me to deposit it for you, I can do that, too."

"That's very kind."

"You lie down," he said. "Point me to the kitchen and I'll heat this up." He held up the bag with the soup in it.

She gestured toward the hall. "I don't have much of an appetite."

"You need to eat. Now sit."

A few minutes later, after scavenging for a bowl to microwave the soup he'd bought from the best deli in Santa Barbara, he served her supper, and brought a bowl for himself.

She seemed grateful, but somehow humbled. "This is so embarrassing. I hate for you to see me like this."

He slurped a taste of broth. "Don't give it another thought. Just eat."

She took a dainty sip and nodded her approval. As she continued to eat, he surreptitiously studied her face. For the first time he noticed a faint butterfly rash across the bridge of her nose and cheeks. Perhaps she was still feverish.

When she'd eaten half the bowl, she cast it aside on the coffee table. "It's very good, but I've eaten so little all week, I've lost my appetite."

"Then I'll be back tomorrow morning with fresh rolls and fluffy eggs."

"I can't let you do that."

"Of course you can. I'm a doctor. Let me help you get better. Now, tell me your symptoms and I'll try to figure out if you need antibiotics or something. I've got my bag in the car; I can give you a check-up if you'd like. And, while I'm out there, I'll bring in more wood for your fire and start this one up again."

"It's Lupus," she broke in.

He stopped his rambling.

"I have Systemic Lupus Erythematosus. I caught an everyday virus, something Gina brought home from pre-school, and now I'm having a flare-up."

That explained the rash on her face. "How long have you had SLE?"

"I developed it after Gina was born. I'd had lots of weird symptoms for years, but I think the post partum hormonal imbalance finally knocked me over the line."

"I had no idea," he said, feeling an overwhelming desire to somehow make her life better. Easier. She'd given no clue that she lived with a chronic autoimmune disease. Especially one that could be as debilitating as Lupus. "You're under a doctor's care?"

She nodded. "I see a Lupus specialist. And I add some complementary herbs to my regimen, too." She offered a wan smile. "Sometimes the cure seems worse than the disease."

No wonder she was such an alternative medicine advocate. Now it all made sense.

Satisfied she was doing the right thing, he relaxed. "Let me make you some tea." He jumped up, wanting nothing more than to wait on her.

He realized, by her obvious hesitation, she probably didn't want any tea, but even when sick, she was gracious.

"There's some chamomile leaves in the cupboard next to the refrigerator," she said in an anemic voice.

Or maybe she was just too weak to protest.

As he went about boiling water he called out, "Where's Gina?"

"With her father."

A pang of guilt made him realize he was relieved he wouldn't see "squirt" on this visit.

"He picked her up this afternoon. The poor thing has been so good about my being sick all week. And my childcare lady has been picking her up every day. She even took her to preschool. Mrs. Densmore has been watching her for a couple of hours in the evenings. I don't know what I would have done otherwise."

The predicament of being a single mother was daunting enough, Jason imagined, but having a chronic illness on top of it seemed unfathomable. Again, he marveled at how he'd never had a clue about Claire's personal plight; how upbeat and cheerful she always seemed. Now that he knew, he'd find a way to help relieve her burden.

They sipped their tea, as Claire stretched out her legs and covered up with the blanket. He resisted tucking in her feet, using the poker to move a log around in the fireplace instead.

"Sometimes it's too much to lift my head off the pillow. Charles couldn't take the thought of living with an invalid, even though I rarely have flare-ups."

"You mean to tell me he divorced you because of your Lupus?"

She nodded, a look of resignation dulling her features. "That and a perky waitress at his favorite harbor bar."

Jason shook his head. As he drank his tea in silence, he thought of his deceased wife and what he'd give to have her back. Then he thought how stupid Claire's husband was for turning his back on her. The Claire he knew at the clinic was vital and witty, feisty and bright, and…*quit denying it*…sexy.

Perky waitress or not, the man obviously didn't know how lucky he'd been being married to a woman like Claire. But Jason didn't know the whole story, so he reserved his full judgment.

Jason hoped Charles was at least good to Gina. If he did anything to hurt her… His blood pressure rose just thinking about the potential. Had he inadvertently transferred his feelings for Hanna to Gina? He hardly knew the child, yet he'd already seemed to form a bond. Didn't he have an art gallery's worth of drawings to prove they were special to each other? He couldn't let that go any further.

A rueful smile creased his lips. Jessica and Hanna would never be a part of his life again, and their loss stained every breath he took with guilt and anguish. A kid like Gina and a woman like Claire only complicated things.

"Are you OK?" Claire asked.

"What?" For crying out loud, he'd come over here to help her feel better, and now she was the one worrying about him. "Oh, I'm fine. I was just thinking of the irony of it all. You're a living breathing woman with a lot to offer, and I think your husband is a fool for leaving you."

She made a weak attempt at a smile. "Thanks.

It's been hard, but things are looking up with the new job and all."

"I'll make sure you get paid sick leave," he said, though usually any new employee needed to work three months before sick leave pay kicked in.

Her feeble smile grew stronger. "For such a grouch, you're a prince. Thanks," she said. He thought he saw a quick glint of life in her eyes, and he was willing to take the cheap shot as a sacrifice.

"*Moi?* A grouch? Are you sure you're not feverish?" He knew damned well he wasn't an easy man to work for, but he was surprised she'd been so candid. That was something else he liked about her. She was honest with him. Hell, hadn't she called him a closed-minded medical robot on her first day at work? That took guts.

He clapped his hands together. "So what time do you prefer breakfast?"

"Honestly, Jason, you don't have to do that."

Their eyes came together. He held her gaze long and sternly. "Don't be a martyr." Wasn't that a bit like the pot calling the kettle black? But he'd made his stand and he wasn't backing down now. "I want to help you, and I make a mean omelet."

She laughed. It sounded more like surrender than joy. "Then I'll have Cheddar cheese with fresh avocado slices on top."

Ha! He might have to get up early to drive to the farmers' market to find a ripe avocado, but he wasn't about to let her know that. "As you wish, my lady." Only because she'd called him a prince did the "my lady" tag occur to him. It sounded completely unnatural, something he'd never say, and he wanted to cringe the moment he'd said it. It felt too intimate and foreign when it slipped out of his mouth, but he'd said it and couldn't take it back. He glanced at Claire, reclining on the sofa looking pale and angelic. Really? Had it felt that foreign to call her "my lady"?

"And sourdough toast," she added, bringing him out of his convoluted, awkward and uneasy thoughts.

"Strawberry preserves?" he said.

"Marmalade, please."

"Hmm. I hadn't pegged you as a marmalade kind of girl."

She forced a smile through her compromised state, and he recognized a trace of the vital woman he'd come to know at the clinic. He stood, crossed the room and straightened the blanket over her feet.

"I'll be here at nine. I'll bring the food. You bring your appetite."

She gazed gratefully into his eyes. "I'll do my best, boss."

"See to it." He stopped himself from patting her shoulder. "I'll let myself out. You get a good night's sleep. That's an order."

As he reached the door he heard a faint, "Thank you."

And, just before he closed the door, he turned. He could go sailing any weekend with the mild local climate, and he would gladly cancel the weekend plans in favor of helping out a sick employee. A new friend? "You're entirely welcome," he said.

A slender arm with graceful hand and fingers waved above the back of the sofa, and a strange feeling came over him.

Was getting more involved with Claire Albright a good idea or a recipe for disaster?

CHAPTER FOUR

CLAIRE didn't want to be a medical burden to anyone but herself. Being sick had ended her marriage, but she also knew if she'd married the right guy he would have stuck it out with her. When Charles had proposed, she'd been positive he was the one for her. He might have been if she hadn't gotten sick. When her illness had developed the real Charles had emerged and, because her heart had been nearsighted, nothing had prepared her for his rejection.

Since then, she'd made a vow to deal with her illness alone.

So why had she allowed Jason to bring breakfast today? Because he seemed to be on her side, and she could use a friend. At least that was how it had felt last night when he'd shown up at her door with her pay check and chicken soup. He'd made an extra effort to stop by and, since she'd been feeling very alone lately, it had touched her.

After taking a shower and forcing herself to get dressed for the first time all week, she felt a lot better. Almost human again. And she wasn't sure if she'd washed and combed her hair for herself or partially for Jason. The notion disturbed her but was a revelation she'd have to deal with when she wasn't sick. She simply didn't have enough energy left now.

She'd decided to wait to take her morning cocktail of medicine until she'd eaten breakfast. And she'd take Jason up on his offer to deposit her check in the bank for her. The thought of running errands seemed overwhelming. Last night, he'd brought the paperwork for her to sign up for automatic deposit, and that thoughtful gesture almost made her cry. How long had it been since someone had looked out for her?

She shook her head. The Lupus flare-up had

weakened her resolve. She'd never depend on anyone but herself again.

Now that she was clean and dressed, she felt as though she needed to take a nap, and it was only a quarter to nine. She plopped onto the couch and stared at the ceiling.

Jason had been a prince to stop by last night. She had barely believed her eyes when she'd opened the door. And he'd appeared genuinely concerned for her. Though she'd been caught looking her worst, she'd been too sick to feel embarrassed about it. Now he knew about her condition. After he fulfilled his obligation to feed her breakfast, she could expect him to back off. No one wanted to be strapped to a chronically sick person. Wasn't that what Charles had finally admitted when she'd had her third relapse in one year?

"Look at you," he'd said. "You're nothing like the woman I married."

Claire remembered examining herself in the mirror thinking she looked the same, but she knew he referred to her fluctuating pain and energy level. He'd made her feel ugly and unwanted, and it had broken her heart.

She shook her head. The steroids always messed with her mind. She definitely hadn't been thinking straight by allowing new feelings to sneak into her life since meeting Jason Rogers. Today, she'd put an end to that.

The knock on her door startled her. She stood and felt light-headed, leaned on the back of the couch and, when he knocked a second time, she straightened and headed on unsteady legs toward the door.

Jason's broad smile surprised her, since he shared it so infrequently. "Welcome back to the living," he said, giving her a once-over. "You look…nice."

"Nice" was a bland description, but it was better than *like a zombie*, and he seemed to need time to think what he wanted to say. He was definitely being polite.

The Saturday morning sunlight made her squint. A rich blue sky with cotton ball clouds had her wishing she could go out to play. He entered the house looking downright debonair in a nautical shirt, khaki Dockers and deck shoes without socks. And the way his hair always fell across his forehead… Well, what could she say, but she liked it. She liked the whole package.

He'd probably deliver the food and run. Saturday was his day off and, from the looks of him, he had a date with his sailboat. She'd seen the picture of the sleek white craft named *Hanna's Haven* on his office wall. And his constant light tan indicated he spent a lot of time outdoors.

Jason barreled through the entryway and headed straight for the kitchen with grocery bags in hand. She followed him. He removed a Thermos, and his eyes brightened.

"I've brought my special breakfast coffee blend. Sit down and relax." He pulled out a chair, and when she sat he scooted a second chair toward her. "Put your feet up." He scanned the cupboards and she pointed to the one that held the mugs. He seemed excited and happy to be here, which took Claire by surprise. Wasn't she merely an obligation he'd inadvertently tied himself to?

Fifteen minutes later, as Claire sipped the richest coffee she'd ever tasted, breakfast was ready. Her eyes widened when he placed a perfect omelet in front of her.

"Are you a chef in your spare time?"

"I've been known to tinker around in the galley, though I haven't done much of that for a while." His bright eyes dimmed and his demeanor changed. He became quiet and joined her at the table.

They ate in silence, Claire forcing herself to clean the plate. How could she not when he'd found a perfectly ripened avocado to top off the light and fluffy egg and cheese dish? With the added calories, Claire felt more energetic. "I'm a pretty good cook, too," she said. "I'll have to pay you back when I get better."

He looked tenderly at her. "I'll hold you to that," he said, as they shared a smile.

Maybe he was just humoring her, but the

glint in his eyes told her otherwise. Claire did feel as if she'd rounded the bend on this flare up, and, if things continued in this forward movement, she could hope to be at work on Monday.

"Some of the surveys have already been returned," he said, mid-bite.

"Great, I can't wait to put the data together."

"I took the liberty to start a spreadsheet of the findings," he said.

"That's wonderful. That will help me a lot."

"I'll give you all the help you need."

She saw sincerity in his blue-flecked eyes. Ever since she'd noticed the distinction, his gray eyes would never be the same to her. That was the steroids thinking. They made her emotional. Logically, she knew theirs was purely a business relationship, but having him here in her kitchen, casually eating and talking around the table, she became aware of a longing she'd pushed away—a longing to connect with another human being.

She had her daughter and her job, she

thought as she took the last bite of omelet, and that would have to be enough.

Monday morning Jason was glad to see Claire at his office door. The second floor had seemed dull and quiet without her, and he'd even admitted to missing the aromatherapy, but not enough to learn how to turn on the diffuser.

Her being here meant she was back on the mend—the most important reason he was glad to see her.

"Good morning," she said, looking a bit pale, but far better than she had the last time he'd seen her.

"How are you feeling?" He jumped up from his chair and joined her at the door.

"Almost a hundred percent. I wanted to thank you again for helping me out."

Jason cupped her arm. "I was glad to do it."

He studied her warm hazel eyes and wondered what thoughts might be tumbling through her mind. Aware of the point of connection and how natural it felt to touch her, he removed his hand. Fortunately she'd worn a blouse with sleeves, though he did wonder how her skin might feel. A flash memory of his wife caused him to retreat to his desk.

If Claire thought his action abrupt or odd, she gave no hint of it. A smile spread across her face, and she held up a paper. "I got your consult request."

"Maybe you can straighten Ms. Garcia out. I give up."

She laughed, and the sound made him think of a babbling brook. It became impossible to stay aloof.

"It's all about keeping a positive attitude, Jason," she said as she wandered back to her office in a flowing gypsy skirt. She'd worn her hair up today and he liked the view of her slender neck above the white lab coat.

His attitude toward Claire had changed over the last few weeks from annoying employee, to useful addition to the practice, to potential friend, and possible… The next thought made the hair on his arms stand on end.

Then he remembered what tomorrow was. He didn't need to look at the calendar to know that it was his daughter's birthday.

His nurse appeared in the doorway with a patient chart and, with the threat of purgatory bearing down on him tomorrow, he was grateful for the distraction of his job.

Tuesday morning Claire arrived at work to find Jason's office door closed. She knew he was there because she'd seen his Mercedes in the parking lot. Something told her not to bother him, and an hour later when they both exited exam rooms at the same time, one look at him and she knew she'd made the right decision.

Jason looked as if he hadn't slept all night. A shadow of his usual self, he hadn't even bothered to shave and his appearance stopped just short of disheveled.

His gaze fused with hers and she saw pain cutting through his stare. On reflex she wanted to reach out to him, to comfort him in some small way from the torment so apparent in his eyes, but the invisible barrier he wore was solid and impenetrable, and she instinctively knew to leave him alone.

She nodded a respectful greeting, wishing she could do much more for him.

He acknowledged her and retreated to his office.

The next day, Claire was elbow-deep in patient surveys—each day brought in another fifty to a hundred of them—and she had high hopes of completing her first report in time for next week's staff meeting. Every flat surface in her office was piled high with the envelopes.

One of the surveys concerned her, and she needed to speak to Jason about his patient. When he walked right by her door and straight to his office without saying hello that morning, she hesitated. Looking over Mrs. Ching's herbal supplements, she couldn't let Jason's somber and standoffish mood hold her back.

She gathered the list and took a deep breath, then headed down the hall.

Claire peeked around the door and tapped on the frame. "May I talk to you?"

Jason had managed to shave today, but the dark circles remained under his eyes. He glanced up and gave a solemn nod.

She swallowed, her throat suddenly dry. How did he manage to make her this nervous without so much as a spoken word?

“I was looking at Mrs. Ching’s survey and discovered she takes several herbs used in Chinese traditional medicine.”

He gave her a blank, uninterested stare as if to say *more holistobabble?*

“The thing is,” she said, “I remember her face being puffy that day when you asked me to look at her back. Especially around the eyes. And I noticed in her chart that her last labs were several months ago.”

“The results were normal.”

“Yes, which makes sense why you haven’t repeated them,” she said, plowing on. “But I’m concerned about some of the supplements she’s taking. I’d like to call her daughter and find out all of the ingredients.”

“You have my permission.” Could he be more aloof?

"And I'd like to order more labs."

He nodded, concentrating on whatever lay on his desk, as if she were nothing more than a small distraction.

Claire thought they'd taken three steps forward over the weekend, but it was only Wednesday and they'd fallen ten steps back, like when she'd first arrived at the medical clinic. It was clear Jason was unreachable today, so she'd remain professional, do her job, and leave the man alone.

Jason had made it through his daughter's birthday for another year. She'd have been eight. Would the pain ever go away? He'd spent last night drinking, combing through her belongings he couldn't bear to part with, and biting back the tears. He'd cursed the world and ranted about the injustice of it all, as he did every year. She should be losing teeth and studying multiplication tables. She should be arguing with her best friend one day and making up the next. She should be his date at the father-daughter school dance. She should be sitting on his lap, letting him spoil her.

She should be alive.

He swiped his jaw. He was at work, and the dreaded day was over. He needed to get a handle on his emotions, but the room went blurry again.

Damn it!

He stepped outside his office to see his next patient and caught the rustle of Claire's turquoise-blue dress as she entered her exam room. He glanced toward her office, which seemed to glow, then back to his dreary room. Hell, he hadn't even bothered to turn on the lights today.

In the waiting room, the gentle scent of lavender and whatever the hell the other essential oil Claire had told him it was, smelled good. He took a long inhalation, and squared his shoulders. He'd survived the hell of Hanna's birthday again, which always led to reliving her last day. He had three months to go before his wife's birthday, where he'd descend back into hell for another day, and then the fourth anniversary of the accident a month after that. God, would it ever get any easier?

He glanced toward Claire's office again. She had her share of obstacles to overcome, yet she always seemed optimistic. There was a quiet strength in her that he respected. Her life hadn't turned out the way she'd expected, the way she'd deserved, yet she kept moving forward and didn't gripe about it.

Existing in limbo was hell. And exhausting. And tedious. Maybe he'd try to join the living and look on the brighter side of life for a change.

Jason packed up his briefcase Friday night. He'd played catch up on labs, special tests and consult reports after the clinic closed rather than go home to an empty house. He planned to pick up some take-out food on the way, then he'd leave before dawn Saturday for an all-day sail.

He missed the soothing sea, the one place where life seemed to make sense to him. The silence and magnitude of the ocean brought him peace of mind: The luffing of the sails before they filled, the creaking and stretching of the rigging, and the water lapping against the topsides. He'd made it through another week at the clinic, and through his daughter's birthday, and he'd reward himself with a day on the water.

Claire appeared in his doorway. "Jason? Mrs. Ching may have Chinese herb nephropathy."

"What?"

She rushed into his office and leaned over his desk. "Her labs show evidence of renal ischemia. She may be toxic. I spoke to her daughter, who said she was taking these herbs for joint aches and pain relief for the last month. One of the ingredients may contain aristolochic acid."

"And I should know this?"

"No," she said, cheeks pink and eyes shining. "I should because I've studied it, but it isn't commonly known. There could have been an inadvertent mix-up in one of the ingredients with this herbal mixture. What should be *A. Fangji*, a harmless herb, could actually be *A. Fangchi* a herb that contains aristolochic acid, which can cause renal failure. Something like this happened a few years back. I remember reading the article."

"What do we do now?"

"I called Mrs. Ching's daughter and told her to stop the herbs immediately—that they could be life-threatening—and I've left a message for her herbalist to call me."

Claire took her job seriously, and had managed to identify a potentially fatal herb interaction for one of his patients.

"Good idea." He smiled at the vibrant woman in front of him.

She blushed and he definitely liked it whenever she did. "So, assuming the worst and you're right and Mrs. Ching can potentially go into renal failure, what do we do next? Are renoprotective agents enough to turn her around?"

"I think we should admit her," she said.

"Treat her like any other nephropathy patient?"

She nodded. "Hopefully, the damage is reversible. In extreme cases, the kidneys and ureters are so damaged, they have to be surgically removed. There's no telling what's going on with her at this point."

He got on the phone and started barking out instructions. "I'm heading over to the Hospital to prepare for Mrs. Ching's admit. You call her and tell her daughter to bring her and meet me there. If she gives you any trouble, I'll personally go to her house and drag her there myself," he said.

"I'd like to come, too," she said.

"Sure."

"Oh, but wait. Gina." Claire tapped her finger on her mouth. "I know! I'll call my landlady and ask if she can watch her. She loves Gina."

Claire grabbed her cellphone and made the calls while following Jason out to the car.

"Mrs. Ching's on her way and Gina gets to have delivery pizza for dinner tonight with Mrs. Densmore. Lucky girl."

They spent the next two hours at the local E.R. having Mrs. Ching admitted, while Jason wrote out a plethora of kidney specific tests to be performed. When he was satisfied he'd covered everything from basic kidney function labs to ultrasound, MRI, IVP, cytoscopy and renal biopsy, he glanced up to find Claire looking over his shoulder. She'd been sick in bed all last week, and here she was one week later, like a trouper sticking by his side while he took care of one of his patients. If it hadn't been for her astute find, Mrs. Ching could have been on the fast track to dialysis or, worse yet, a nephrectomy.

Claire looked a little drawn and her stomach made a gurgling plea about the missed dinner hour.

"Excuse me," she said as she grabbed her waist, color rising on her cheeks.

"Let's get some dinner," he said.

She opened her mouth, but he didn't give her the chance to protest.

"I owe you," he said. "It's the least I can do."

"Well, since you put it that way…let me call my landlady and ask if it's OK with her."

Claire snapped her cellphone closed with a smile on her face. "Now they're watching a

Disney video, and Gina's already in her pajamas. She'll be happy to tuck her in bed for me."

"That's great."

A half hour later they were being seated at Aldo's, his favorite Italian restaurant on State Street. He ordered a bottle of Chianti and, while they waited for their pasta dinner for two, they drank wine and relaxed.

Without her lab jacket on, her peach-colored crinkly top brought out all of the finest aspects of her complexion. Her eyes looked more green than hazel tonight, and she gave him an inquisitive glance as he watched her sip her drink. He'd noticed her mouth on several occasions, but hadn't allowed himself to study the fullness of her lips. They looked smooth and soft and he wondered what it would be like to kiss them.

The wine had obviously gone right to his head, and when the waiter brought out the fresh baked bread he slathered a piece with butter and took a large bite. Anything to get his mind off her mouth.

"You like to sail?" she asked.

"It's my passion. Nothing like it in the world. You?"

"I've never had the opportunity to try it."

He told her about the summer he hired on as a deck hand on a schooner and sailed all the way to Hawaii, and how he'd owned his first sloop by the age of twenty-one. It had been a birthday gift from his parents for finishing his pre-med courses a year early. His current schooner, *Hanna's Haven*, had been a gift to himself when he'd passed the family practice boards.

He'd wanted to spend his honeymoon sailing around the Caribbean but Jessica hadn't been a natural born sailor, and they'd flown there instead. He didn't tell Claire *that* part of the story and, while he ate more pasta, he pondered how all the roads in his life seemed to lead back to Jessica.

In turn, Claire told him about her upbringing in Los Angeles, how she'd wanted to be a gymnast when she was little, but had grown too tall and had turned out to be a bit clumsy, and since she couldn't cut it as a gymnast had decided she'd become a nurse. She finished by telling him how she'd gone to Santa Barbara University and could never get herself to move back home after that.

And after a satisfying dinner following a strained and uncomfortable week, they looked at each other in a different light, more on the lines of the prior weekend when they'd forged new ground, established respect for each other, and become unlikely friends.

"You seemed to have a rough week," Claire said, running her finger around the edge of her almost-empty wine glass.

"I've had worse. I'm OK now."

"If you ever want to talk about it," she said, "I'd be glad to listen."

He nodded, feeling the Chianti warm his chest. With his hunger satisfied, and no desire to open up about himself, Jason suggested they walk up the street for ice cream. That way he wouldn't have to keep gazing into her empathetic, appealing eyes.

"I think after tonight I'll have made up for all

the weight I lost when I was sick," she said as they strolled.

He glanced from her head to her open-toed shoes. She always painted her toenails, and he liked that. She wore beige slacks instead of her usual skirt or dress and, though a little thin, for the first time he noticed how nicely shaped she was. "That's not a bad thing, is it?"

Jason knew that figuring out the female psyche and ideal weight was beyond his capabilities, so he trod lightly.

She laughed, and there was that babbling brook image again. He smiled at her, grateful she hadn't taken offense on any level, and they continued to walk up State Street on the brisk but clear evening.

Maybe tonight, for just one night, he could forget…

Claire glanced at Jason as they ambled up the red-brick walk toward the ice cream store. She'd learned more about him tonight, yet still felt he was mostly a stranger. He never seemed to completely open up, and it made her think he was an emotionally unavailable man. That was the last thing she was looking for. She'd been married to one, and look how horribly that had turned out. She'd never repeat the same mistake.

This was just dinner with a business associate. They'd admitted their patient and had been hungry. It only made sense he'd ask her to eat with him. So why was she making more out of it than it was?

Because the restaurant had been cozy and romantic, with white tablecloths and dim candlelight. Because the conversation had come easy and she'd kept getting lost in his ocean-at-dusk-colored eyes. Because she couldn't deny it any longer—she was attracted to Jason. He was a skilled and dedicated doctor who loved his patients. Unbeknownst to her, he'd been the force behind the medical group that she'd discovered in the renovated Victorian house, the place where she'd yearned to work. He was kind to her daughter.

And he'd proved to be a concerned business partner when he'd gone the extra mile last Friday night to bring her pay check, and he'd surprised her even more with a gourmet breakfast Saturday morning.

Chianti or no Chianti, she found him extremely attractive, even liked the way he talked, with his deeper than average voice. He had a wide smile when he cared to share one with her, and masculine lips, the kind that had made her mind wander to kissing when he'd told her about sailing. She found it fascinating how his beard had darkened as the day progressed into the evening, was glad she'd been around to notice, and surprised to realize she wanted to touch the stubble.

He glanced at her and tilted his head with an inquisitive expression when he realized she'd been studying him. Again.

Thankfully, they'd reached the ice cream store because her line of thinking needed to stop.

"How should we work this?" Jason asked later, after scooping up the last of his ice cream from the small foam cup. "Should I drive you back to the clinic to get your car, or should we buy Gina a mini ice cream and take it right to her?"

"That's sweet of you, but no. It would just get her all wired. You can take me back to my car. What she doesn't know won't hurt her feelings. But thanks for thinking about her." His small, yet considerate gestures kept adding up, and it made him hard to resist.

Fifteen minutes later he'd parked in the medical clinic lot and something told Claire to be still. Jason didn't make a move to get out of the car; he stared straight ahead for a few moments, and she could hear each breath he took. Then he turned toward her. "I can't remember the last time I asked a woman out to dinner."

She wanted to brush off his statement. To say *oh, I'm just a business associate, we were working late and got hungry*, but she didn't want to believe that. And he'd hinted that he'd made a point of asking her to dinner. He didn't have to. It complicated things, and she opted to keep the mood light by mocking herself.

"I'm glad you did," she said, "even if I had to go to great lengths to figure out a way to get a patient to take toxic herbs, and get hospitalized, in order to get you to ask me." She grinned.

He grinned back. "So this was all your devious plan," he deadpanned.

"Oh, yes. I thought of everything."

His smile slipped away as his steady gaze melded with hers. "Then I'm glad, too."

She couldn't fight the growing attraction, even though it was the last thing in the world she needed right now. She also considered herself good at reading people—a natural ability that she'd enhanced with her homeopathy studies—and, by the look on Jason's face, he seemed deeply interested in her, too.

He leaned toward her. With the smoky tinge to his eyes, she knew what he planned.

Before she had a chance to think one extra thought, his mouth covered hers. The lips she'd wondered about were warm and smooth, and they fit perfectly over hers. She relaxed and let him take the lead, enjoying the feel of him.

Though waning, the sandalwood scent of his aftershave still invited her closer. He slowly pulled back, but she wanted more. She followed his mouth and pressed her moistened lips to his and, to keep him from retreating more, her hand caressed his jaw and neck. His ear was warm and she finally got to test the stubble on his cheek. She didn't detect any resistance from him when she kissed him again.

She loved the sounds they made when their lips parted to kiss again and again. He kissed her lower lip, and tugged on it, and sleepy sensations tugged in other areas of her body. His hand found her back and he drew her closer. They breathed over each other; she sighed, and kissed him harder. He deepened the kiss, making it moist and silky. Their tongues met and a tiny sound escaped her throat. He must have liked it. His hand kneaded her back as their tongues continued to test and explore. Her fingers splayed into his hair. It was thick and newly trimmed across his neck. She wanted more kisses and planted several of her own as a sensual awareness started to throb deep within her.

And then he ended it. He abruptly dropped his hand and backed away from her mouth. A complicated expression shadowed his face. Was he appalled by what they'd done, or just not into her?

All she knew was that she missed his warmth. She missed how his barriers had tumbled down as they'd kissed, and how he'd pulled her tight, inviting her to know him a little deeper with each kiss.

But it was over now. He was back to staring out the car windshield, and she felt obligated to say something. She didn't want to make a single comment about the kisses, preferring to hoard them rather than allow him to steal them back with an apology or an excuse. They were real and they'd felt wonderful. One second he'd been warm and inviting, the next his lips had turned to marble and he'd disappeared.

The kiss probably didn't mean a thing to him. It was just a bit of extra-curricular activity on his part, and she'd taken it too seriously. It served her right for breaking her own rule about getting involved with a man again. How easily Jason had persuaded her to reconsider that vow.

Claire reached for the door handle and opened the door. "Thank you for dinner, Jason. I really enjoyed myself." Even after scolding herself, she still hoped he'd hear the double message. How messed up was that?

He turned slowly to face her. Night shadows slanted across his jaw, making it hard for her to read his expression. "You're welcome," was all he said, with a distant stare.

Jason watched Claire get into her car; his hands gripped the steering wheel in a lifesaving strangle. What the hell had he done?

He'd come out of hibernation; let his guard down enough to enjoy Claire's company. He'd noticed her sensual mouth, enjoyed every second of their shared kisses, discovered he wanted to ravage her, then the dark thoughts had returned. How could he be unfaithful to Jessica? To this day, her memory wouldn't let go of him. And his guilt would never let him forget.

Claire had managed to find the dwindling spring of life at the bottom of his well. He'd been bone-dry until then, and she'd tapped into what was left of him. Made him feel almost human again. He'd wanted more; had that been so awful?

He was supposed to have been with Jessica and Hanna the day of the accident, but the new medical clinic had delayed him. *Go ahead,* he'd said over the cellphone. *I'll drive up later and meet you there.* They'd planned a weekend in Pismo Beach.

He didn't deserve to be alive, or to feel, or to enjoy anything.

He wouldn't slip up again.

CHAPTER FIVE

MONDAY morning, Claire and René had the medical clinic kitchen to themselves.

René poured herself a large cup of coffee; her full-bodied auburn hair was styled in layers and rested on the white of her doctor's coat, and Claire admired how she always looked perfectly put together. She'd alluded to Jason's troubled past in prior conversations, and after Claire had fruitlessly racked her brain all weekend over the cause of Jason's odd behavior, she needed some answers.

Her divorce had left her wary of men, and maybe the same had happened to Jason, though he never made reference to his ex-wife, as most divorced men did.

They'd had a great dinner together, she'd realized how much she liked him, and he'd kissed her. Then he'd stopped. From one moment to the next, things had changed. Was she a bad kisser? Or had Jason had a sudden change of heart about her?

Something had kept Claire from writing Jason off as another of life's disappointments wrapped in a male package. She needed to know the whole story before she did that. She sat beside René and dipped her tea ball in the steaming mug of water.

"You have a minute?" she asked.

"Of course. What's up?" René's amber-brown eyes reminded her of a cat's.

"I can't figure Jason out. He's a grouch one minute, kind the next. Did you know that he brought me soup and my pay check when I was sick?"

René's perfectly made-up eyes widened and her brows rose halfway up her forehead. "Jason brought you soup?"

Claire nodded, with a wan smile at the memory. The man thoroughly confused her.

"He did seem to ask a lot of questions about where you were and what was wrong when you were out sick."

The notion of Jason worrying about her caused a warm sensation in her chest.

René tilted her head in thought. After several moments and a sip of coffee, she looked Claire in the eyes. "Jason used to be the life of the party. He had more charm than the President," she said. "His family is filthy rich, in case you didn't know, and he never wanted for anything. He was a devoted family man. Completely content. And a great doctor. Still is a great doctor, just a little less accessible on the personal level." René glanced at Claire with a rueful expression.

"Did he get divorced?"

René shook her head. "These days, he's just doing the best he can." She looked as if she wanted to say more, but before she could her nurse stuck her head around the door.

"Dr. Munroe? Mrs. Callahan is on the phone. She thinks she's in labor."

René popped up from her chair. "Looks like my day has officially begun. We'll talk more later."

Claire shook her head. If he wasn't divorced, then what was he?

She'd give Jason some space for now but, having recently been introduced to his passion for the sea, she couldn't let him continue to sail at half mast. He needed a friend. And if they were going to be friends, he needed to talk. She shook her head, knowing there was no way she could force him to open up and talk. The man was so closed off; he'd probably never bring the subject up. But he'd shown early signs of life at dinner the other night, and there had been passion in his kiss. And she did owe him a dinner.

A relationship was probably the last thing he needed. Or wanted. Come to think of it, it was the last thing she needed, too. They could be friends, and together, as *friends*, they might find a place for him to begin to live again.

And if she were lucky, through that friendship, maybe she could learn to trust again, too.

After a few more moments lost in thought,

Claire scrubbed her face with her palms, finished her tea, and set off for her first physical exam of the day.

Breaking through to Jason and becoming his friend seemed too much to ask for, but she'd never shied away from challenges in her life. Why start now?

As the morning wore on Claire's insecurity got the best of her. How was she supposed to go about this? *Hi, I'm Claire. Can I be your friend because I think you need one, and I have the audacity to think I can help you?* Ridiculous. She couldn't even help herself get over her lack of trust. What made her think she could offer Jason anything?

She wound up being a coward and avoided him the rest of the morning.

He'd made it easy by staying in his office with his door closed in between patients. She kicked herself for not having any guts, but just before the end of the morning clinic, she had a perfect excuse to tap on his door.

But Jason's door was open, and she needed to borrow his more up-to-date drug formulary, so she went inside. She glanced around the bookcase to locate the bright orange 2010 handbook, when her gaze settled on a small picture. A lovely dark-haired woman and a little girl with impish eyes smiled out at her from the delicate frame. They had to be the family René had referred to.

What had happened?

Jason barreled into the room and tossed some paperwork on his desk. Startled, Claire almost dropped the picture.

"Oh," she said. "I was just looking for your drug formulary."

"And you decided to snoop while you were in the neighborhood?" He pinned her with an accusatory glare.

"I'm sorry, Jason. I just happened to notice this lovely picture and…"

He walked to another bookcase across from his desk and flipped out the item in question. "Is this what you're looking for?"

At a total loss for what else to say, she nodded. "Yes. Thank you." She took the book and retreated to her office, feeling humiliated and angry, and avoided Jason the rest of the afternoon. The man's barriers were thicker than steel trapdoors.

Frustrated by an afternoon that had seemed to yawn on, Claire arrived home with a bag of groceries and Gina in tow to find a message on her answering machine from her landlady, Mrs. Densmore.

"*Claire, I'm not doing well. Can you check in on me?*"

A chill cut through Claire. Mrs. Densmore never complained about anything. Though frail, she was still one of those robust North-eastern transplants who laughed at the spoiled mild climate residents of California, and who could be seen gardening in the foulest coastal weather. Her violet-colored hydrangeas, lipstick-red hibiscus, and cross-bred multi-colored roses were proof positive of her green thumb. She walked daily with a fancy carved walking stick, and scoffed at people who rushed to the doctor for little problems. Only something major would cause her to ask for help.

Claire put the groceries that needed refrigeration away, and left the rest. She gave Gina some wheat crackers and string cheese, took her by the hand and rushed to Mrs. Densmore's door. It seemed like ages before the woman answered.

On the surface Mrs. Densmore looked her usual self, except she hadn't bothered to pull her shock of white hair back in a bun. It hung thin and limply on her hunched up shoulders. Her face seemed stiff, dried drool clung to the corners of her mouth, where a peculiar grin contradicted her plea for help. No, this wasn't at all like the normal Mrs. Densmore.

"I'm sick," she said. "I thought it was flu. It's something else."

"Do you want me to take you to the urgent care or E.R.?" Claire asked, trying to hide her alarm.

"I don't want to go there. Can you examine me?"

Now was not the time to argue with someone

about their being stubborn. Her landlady needed her help.

Gina wanted to hug Mrs. Densmore the way she always did. Claire bent down to make eye-to-eye contact with her. "Mrs. Densmore is sick, Gina. I need you to be good."

Gina's wide blue eyes stared at the older lady. "She thick? I be good." With that, she walked across the room, patted Mrs. Densmore's hand, then crawled up on her favorite antique rocking chair and started it in motion. "Where you hurt?"

Mrs. Densmore didn't respond to Gina, a child she normally showered with attention, and Claire knew the woman needed medical attention.

She cleared her head and opened her nursing bag. Normally, she didn't do home visits, especially when casual acquaintances were trying to tap her for an easy diagnosis. The liability issue was an entirely different matter. But her landlady wasn't like that.

She listened to Mrs. Densmore's list of complaints: back pain, generalized stiffness, and jaw pain for the last week, which had been getting progressively worse. Heart attacks presented with non-traditional symptoms in women. She needed to rule that out. Or a stroke.

"Have you lost consciousness at any time?" Claire asked, and noted the woman's head shake. "Are you sure?"

Mrs. Densmore gave a sharp stare in answer.

"Give me your hands. Squeeze mine." Mrs. Densmore's grip was equal on both sides. Normally she'd ask a patient to smile to help check for stroke, but the odd grin was already in place. And she'd had a steady even gait.

Claire did a head to toe assessment. Mrs. Densmore's heart rate and rhythm were normal, and so was her blood pressure. Her lungs sounded clear, though it seemed hard for her to take in a deep breath. When Claire got to the woman's hands, she saw several scratches and one angry, swollen cut on her middle finger.

"Gardening," Mrs. Densmore said. "Those

stubborn roses." It seemed difficult for her to talk and swallow.

Gardening. Cuts. Generalized stiffness. Facial spasm. A stubborn woman who avoided the doctor. Mrs. Densmore had recently cleared out a new area in the overgrown back yard. The soil hadn't been disturbed in decades. A dismal thought unnerved Claire. Anaerobic spores in old soil.

"When was the last time you had a tetanus shot?"

The woman made a *pfft* sound, as if to say *Those silly little things?*

Claire didn't want to make a snap decision, but she had a horrendous feeling that her landlady might be in the early stages of tetanus. But who in the world got tetanus these days? Claire had read a recent article in a geriatric journal about an increased incidence of tetanus in elderly gardeners and, if her memory served her right, the older the patient the higher the fatality rate.

"I'm taking you to the E.R.," Claire said.

"No. I won't go."

"You may have had a heart attack or maybe it's tetanus!"

"You don't know that for sure. You're not a doctor."

Mrs. Densmore's traditional and outdated views surprised Claire, but she wasn't about to argue with the woman in her time of need.

"Then I'll get one." And though she'd been a coward all day and had avoided Jason at work, she was worried enough on Mrs. Densmore's behalf to dig into her purse, fish out her cell-phone, locate his number and speed dial it.

"Jason? I need your help. My landlady wants a doctor's input before she'll let me take her to the E.R." Claire gave a frustrated glare at her stubborn landlady. "Where she belongs."

When Jason offered to come right over instead of brushing her off, Claire was both surprised and relieved. He may have clicked into concerned doctor mode, but it hadn't made her any less upset with him for being such a jerk earlier.

"How long ago did you get those scratches?" she asked, focusing back on her patient.

"A week or so, but I get scratched up all the time." The woman looked at her wounded hands, then at Claire. Fear sparked in her eyes. "I started having trouble swallowing today," she said in a confessional voice. "That's why I called you."

Claire rushed to her side and put an arm around her. "If Dr. Rogers says you need to go to the hospital, please don't fight him. OK?"

A tinge of regret crossed over Mrs. Densmore's face. "I know you know what you're doing. It's just that I'm afraid to go to the doctor. When Gerald went, he never came home."

Claire found and handed her a tissue to wipe the brimming tears.

"Medicare can only pay for so much, then you're on your own," Mrs. Densmore said. "They wanted to take our house. It's all I have left." The Densmores had never had children. The woman didn't have a family support system that Claire knew of.

"I'll pay for whatever your insurance doesn't. Don't sweat it." A sharp pang of empathy had Claire making a promise she wasn't sure she could keep. Hell, she could hardly handle her own finances. If she had to, she'd moonlight somewhere in order to help Mrs. Densmore.

Jason must have flown instead of driven because it seemed that only ten minutes later he banged on the mansion door.

Gina ran across the tiled foyer. "Man," she said with a squeal, pointing to Jason when Claire opened the door.

He crouched beside her. "Hey, squirt. What's new?"

Gina jumped up and down. "I drawed you pictures."

"And they were pretty," he said.

"Pwetty." Gina ran around in circles to show her delight. "Pwetty!"

Though distracted at first, Claire and Jason greeted each other cautiously. She thought she'd noticed a hint of contrition in his expression, but he didn't apologize. Claire was grateful to see him and, since they were both focused on a medical condition, none of the awkward fallout she'd imagined there'd be after their first kiss and his subsequent jerk attack at work existed.

Less than fifteen minutes later, he'd convinced Mrs. Densmore where she needed to be. They got the woman into his car and decided that Claire would stay home with Gina.

Jason backed the silver Mercedes sedan out of the circular driveway. "I'll talk to you later," he said.

By eight o'clock, Claire had fed and bathed Gina, read her a goodnight story, and put her to bed. She'd changed into more comfortable clothing—navy-blue velvet warm ups—and fed Mrs. Densmore's litter of cats, then tried to catch up on her *Holistic Health* journal reading, though she had trouble concentrating. By quarter to ten she thought about calling Jason, but didn't want to interfere if he was still at the E.R.

At 10:00 p.m. she heard tapping at her door and reacted with static electricity on her arms and up her neck.

There he stood, hair across his brow, looking depleted but with enough energy to engage her with a single earnest glance. "You were right," he said with half a smile. He followed her into the living room, took off his jacket and laid it over the back of couch, then sat. She joined him on the opposite end, aware of his after-shave and evening stubble.

"So what do they do now?" she asked.

"They've already started her on tetanus immunoglobulin and transferred her to the ICU."

Claire flopped against the cushions. "Can you believe it? Tetanus in this day and age?"

"You've done another terrific job of diagnosing," he said with admiration in his eyes.

It made her want to smile, but she curled her toes instead. "You look tired. Would you like some chamomile tea?"

"Sounds good," he said, "but first I owe you an apology."

"I wasn't snooping, Jason."

"I know that. I'm sorry I snapped at you."

She stared at him for a long moment, and sensed his sincerity. "Apology accepted." She stopped herself from saying—*tell me about that picture. Where are they? What happened to them?* "Why don't you make yourself comfortable while I get that tea."

He kicked off his shoes and put his feet up on her coffee table, and it surprised her. Maybe he'd relax and finally open up.

On the way to the kitchen, she felt jittery and excitable, as if she'd injected a pot of coffee into her veins. Jason had done that to her. She fished around for some cookies to serve with the tea. Why had he chosen to come in person instead of call?

She wouldn't waste the chance to talk to him. Who knew if she'd ever have another opportunity?

Jason had put his hands behind his head and closed his eyes when she returned. They opened shortly after she entered the room.

"It's been a long day," she said.

He responded with a sleepy smile and, fighting off a yawn, he reached for a chocolate chip cookie. "My favorite," he said. "How d'you know?" His eyes teased her as he crunched.

She curled into the corner of the couch and faced him, teacup in hand. Now that Mrs. Densmore was under the appropriate care, she wondered how to broach the other subject foremost on her mind: her new quest for friendship with Jason.

"While I'm apologizing for things, I guess I owe you an explanation for the other night, too," he said.

She almost spilled her tea, but quickly gathered her thoughts and decided to take a huge risk. "And I'd like to know about your family."

He scrubbed his face, and stared hard across the room, as though at nothingness, for several long moments.

"Ten years ago I married my wife, Jessica."

His voice sounded monotone and guarded. "Two years later we had Hanna. You found their picture today. They were the light of my life, as the cliché goes. We talked about having more children, but it never happened. Thought maybe the summer would be a good time to try again." He paused and took a deep breath. "When the clinic opened Phil, Jon, René and I vowed to give it our undivided attention. We worked hard and long at seeing extra patients, hoping word would get out and we'd pick up more clientele. So Jessica and I decided we needed a weekend away. We wanted to do something Hanna would enjoy. She was four, so we made plans to take the train up the coast. But I got held up at work."

He squinted hard at the fire, as if visualizing something horrible.

"I told them to go ahead. That I'd meet them up there." He stopped, his brows twisted, and he pinched his lips together as if fighting off a wave of emotion.

Claire's line of thinking jumped ahead. She remembered a horrendous train crash four or five years ago. She remembered seeing the human carnage amidst twisted metal and derailed train cars on the local TV news. Fifty people had died that day. Her heart squeezed, trying to fathom Jason's pain. She wanted to lunge for him, to throw her arms around his neck and cry with him, but he wasn't shedding a tear. He sat as if numbed by the memories. As if oddly removed from the story that had once been a dark and tragic reality.

He glanced toward her with haunted, weary eyes. "I was supposed to be with them."

Claire's throat tightened, making it difficult to swallow her tea. She couldn't believe what she'd heard. In one instant his family had been wiped out. How could anyone deal with such loss? He seemed to stare right through her. She didn't know what to do. Her hand shot for his. "Jason, I'm so sorry."

A lump clogged Claire's chest. She found it hard to breathe. She thought about the precious gift of her child, and wondered what she would do. She couldn't survive if Gina died.

And Jason had lost both his wife and child.

He moved his hand. "Don't."

She thought of how he'd gazed gently at Gina when she'd fallen asleep in his lap that time, and she wanted to cry. What must he have been thinking? Without knowing it, she'd probably caused him more grief.

He put his shoes back on, grabbed his coat and headed for the door.

She rushed to beat him there and, not giving a damn about what his rules were, hugged him, long and tight. She buried her head under his chin and snuggled against his chest, wanting only to show him he wasn't alone in this world. He may have lost the most precious part of his life, but he wasn't alone.

Instead of being embarrassed about it, she was glad she'd kissed him with her soul Friday night. He deserved no less. And he'd taken a risk with her by reaching out. It touched her. Made her wish things could be different.

He felt rigid and unreceptive, like a man too proud to let anyone help. What a pair they made. She who'd never allow herself to trust a man again, and he who'd never let another woman into his heart.

She gradually disengaged from the one-sided hug.

"I won't tolerate your pity, Claire," he said, then left.

His warning took her by surprise, as if he'd pushed her against a wall. She stared at him as he walked away, and heat rose up her cheeks.

"No more than I'd accept yours!" she called out before he got into his car. A ball of anger and confusion twined around her as she slammed the door with shaky hands.

Tuesday morning, Claire went into work early to make calls to patients who were taking herbs that interacted negatively with their current prescribed medications. She'd chosen to call patients she knew worked and were up early. This way she'd have time in the evening to visit Mrs. Densmore. She heard Jason's footsteps up the stairs and her heart stumbled over the next beat. He stopped outside her door. Turned his head and nodded a greeting.

"Hello, Jason," she said, as casually as her thrumming pulse would allow.

"What are you doing here so early?"

She explained why she'd come in and he stepped inside her office. "Give me some of those," he said, reaching for her pile of surveys.

"You don't have to help."

He tossed her an impatient glance and grabbed half the stack on his way out the door.

As she shook her head at the empty doorway, she heard him step into the waiting room and fiddle with something. Was he turning on the diffuser for the aromatherapy?

A few minutes later when the scent of lavender, ylang-ylang and rosemary wafted up her nose, she smiled in disbelief while she made her next phone call.

Throughout the day, in between her patient appointments, she cogitated over how to reach out to Jason, how to be his friend. He wasn't looking for a replacement for his wife, and she didn't want to ever depend on a man again—theirs seemed like an ideal friendship. Except her body always reacted in unexpected ways whenever he was near, and she was confused about desiring him as a man while settling for a tame friendship. It seemed such a shame to let a good man like Jason live life as a zombie. But if he continued to shut her out of his personal life, all she would have was their business relationship.

She wanted more. The thought sent her sitting back in her chair. She was kidding herself about only wanting friendship with Jason. If she analyzed further, this desire to be friends with Jason was her way of working up the confidence to trust a man again. She shook her head. Of all the men in the entire world to get involved with, Jason seemed the least likely candidate.

That evening at the hospital ICU, Claire was surprised to see that her landlady had been intubated. Claire reached for her hand and squeezed when she arrived. Mrs. Densmore's anxious flitting eyes found Claire and blinked with questions.

Her nurse explained that reflex muscle spasms were causing respiratory compromise, and they planned to perform a tracheotomy the next day. She said they intended to use neuromuscular blocking medications and Mrs. Densmore needed to be mechanically ventilated.

The thought of Gerald Densmore going to the hospital and never coming home had been enough to make her delay seeking medical advice. She could only imagine what was going through her landlady's mind now.

Claire got close to her face. "You are going to pull through this. I know you will." She held both of her hands and squeezed. "I'm taking care of the cats, so don't worry." The irony of a woman who'd avoided the doctor all her life, only to wind up in the ICU in such distress, didn't go unnoticed by Claire, and she suspected it was all that Mrs. Densmore thought about while lying in the bed staring at the ceiling.

Wednesday Claire worked like a fiend to complete her initial herbal supplement survey, and gave the "What to Expect When Nursing" class for René's pregnant clients in the morning. After, she called the hospital and found out Mrs. Densmore's procedure had gone well, and she was stable.

In the afternoon, she facilitated the "Stop Smoking Now" class for Phil's pulmonary patients. When the memo came across her desk about the staff meeting on Thursday night, Claire worked even faster to finish the survey. Unfortunately for the other doctors, Gina would again be taking the meeting along with them.

Gina brought her brand-new board book, *Find the Puppy*, along when Claire picked her up from the sitter's Thursday evening before the staff meeting. She'd also drawn another picture for Jason. They'd spent no less than five minutes rehearsing how to say his name.

This time, they arrived early enough for Claire to feed Gina some finger sandwiches and apple slices before the meeting began.

Jon was the first to arrive, looking as though

he'd just completed a mini marathon in a damp T-shirt, warm-up pants and running shoes with huge soles. He'd been known to hit the beach-side trail during his lunch hour for a quick run, but today he must have gone after the clinic had closed. It was no secret he was training for the May marathon in Los Angeles and, for a man his age, he looked in tip-top condition.

Phil swaggered in next, looking ready for a hot date in dark slacks and a thin baby-blue, long-sleeved v-neck cashmere sweater that brought out his dreamy eyes. In comparison to Jon, he smelled great!

René and Jason arrived together. They spoke casually and laughed like old friends. Claire was surprised by the spike of jealousy that came over her.

Everyone greeted each other, and Jason's eyes met Claire's for a brief moment before he called the meeting to order, causing a quick release of butterflies in her stomach.

As with the last meeting, each member had their specific area of clinic business to report on.

When it was Claire's turn she was prepared with her spreadsheet and several surprising revelations about their clientele and herb-drug interactions.

"Though drug-to-drug interactions are usually more serious, many herbs can interfere with or create potential hazards for our patients," she said. "For example, we know that grapefruit juice can cause abnormally high concentrations of certain drugs in the blood because it inhibits a specific liver enzyme. And did you know that some patients take grapefruit concentrate pills from the health store?"

She looked around the table and noticed a few raised eyebrows.

"We know to warn our patients on those specific medications to avoid grapefruit and grapefruit juice, but can we trust they'll put two and two together about the Pill? And if we don't know that our patient is taking, let's say Goldenseal, when we prescribe them erythromycin for an infection, they may experience toxicity." She glanced around the room, and found everyone, including Jason, to be listening intently. Fortunately, Gina was just as intent drawing yet another picture for her new favorite person—Jason. "And it's also important to be aware some herbs can greatly reduce the effectiveness of our prescribed medications."

To conclude her report, she passed around her list of common herbs and potential drug interactions. "I'd like to make sure that every patient receives this flyer at each medical appointment to remind them to check with their doctor before starting a new herb. And I'd also like to say a word on behalf of the benefits of supplementing medical care with herbs. It has helped tremendously with my battle with Lupus. So herbs aren't by any means all bad. We just have to stay on top of things where our clinic patients are concerned."

"Thanks for this," Jason said, speaking for the group. "How is the survey coming along?"

"We've got a few stragglers who have yet to send back their information. I'd like permission to work a few extra hours Saturday morning to call each of them and encourage them to fill them out and send them in."

All the doctors nodded their approval.

At some point, during her presentation, Gina had wandered over to Jason and crawled into his lap again. He didn't seem to mind. When Gina heard the trigger word, Saturday, she parroted Claire's promise made earlier that evening.

"We go to park on Saturday."

She'd forgotten! Now she'd promised to work Saturday, and Gina would be very disappointed.

All the other doctors had left, and Claire smiled ruefully at Jason.

"I totally forgot about taking Gina to play at the park Saturday." Before Claire could say another word, Gina broke in.

She jumped up and down. "Da park! Thwings." She clapped her chubby hands.

"Maybe we can go on Sunday, honey," Claire said, using her calming mother voice to help ward off the inevitable Hurricane Gina.

The child screwed up her face in preparation for crocodile tears. "Thwings," she cried.

Jason tossed Claire an exasperated glance, then got down to Gina's level and cupped her arms. He gazed into her big blue eyes. Without meaning to, Claire had put him on the spot. "I'll take you to the park on Saturday so Mommy can work. OK?"

"Oh, Jason, you don't have to do that."

"You said so yourself, this survey is very important to the clinic, and the sooner we complete it the better," he said.

"But what about your weekend off?"

"I've got to see my hospitalized patients in the morning, but I'm free in the afternoon, if squirt here can hold her horses."

Gina looked to Claire to help her figure out what that meant. "Dr. Rogers will take you to the park after you eat lunch," she said.

"Better yet," Jason said, "I'll take you to lunch, too."

Gina looked at Claire again, excitement brewing in her eyes. "Yay! Da park."

"Yay, the park," Claire said, as she clapped her hands along with Gina. Now all she had to do was figure out a way to get him to stay for dinner.

CHAPTER SIX

CLAIRE brushed her hair and put the finishing touches to her make-up on Saturday afternoon. Though she'd worn her new aqua-blue blouse, she threw on her favorite threadbare jeans to give the impression she hadn't planned everything, down to the slivered almonds on fresh steamed green beans.

Not only had Jason agreed to take Gina to the park, but to the zoo, too. The Santa Barbara Zoo was a small and perfect place for a pint-sized person to visit.

Claire knew the last thing Jason wanted was to be pitied, and she didn't pity him. She hurt for him; she'd seen the fallout from his misfortune and wanted to offer her friendship. He deserved to salvage his life from the tragedy that had annihilated his family.

The fact that his mere presence gave her crazy thoughts about kissing and touching was something she'd have to deal with another time. Her emotionally unavailable ex-husband had cured her of ever wanting to get involved with a man who'd withhold his heart, for whatever reason, noble or not. And when a man did that, wasn't that the first step toward making it easier to walk away when things got tough? No matter how much her body reacted to Jason, she would guard her heart from any more pain.

The man deserved a friend. And he'd done a very big favor for her today.

The dinner was a chance to get to know Jason better and to ease him back into the world of the living, hopefully without him even realizing it. She had a big job on her hands, but her famous beef stroganoff and made-from-scratch apple pie should do wonders to break through some of his barriers.

The way to a man's heart, as the old saying goes…

No! Not his heart. She brushed the thought from her mind.

The doorbell alerted Claire that, even though she didn't feel quite ready for them, Gina and Jason had arrived home. She took a deep breath, hoping she could pull off her well-planned faux spur-of-the-moment dinner.

"Dock-to Wah-durs took me to the zooooo!" Gina hugged Claire's knees and squealed. "I saw Gemina! Her neck is hurt." She went into a play-by-play description of the giraffe with the crooked neck who was twenty-one-years old, then talked about all the animals she'd seen and imitated the sounds they made. Jason stood quietly as he closed the door, watching Gina's delight with a serious expression.

Claire met his gaze and she could see a hint of sadness. "The zoo was one of Hanna's favorite places," he said in a guarded tone.

Claire's shoulders slumped and she fought the urge to hug him.

"Something smells fantastic," he said, in an obvious attempt to change the subject.

"Oh, it's just one of those candles that smell like homemade apple pie," she said, picking up Gina and delivering a huge kiss to her cheek. "And the other candle just happens to smell like beef stroganoff."

He sniffed the air. "Amazing. And you've got a fresh baked rolls candle, too?"

She blurted a laugh, then grew serious. "Actually, I was hoping I could repay you with a home-cooked meal for bringing me food and fixing me breakfast when I was sick, and especially for helping me out today."

"I'd have to be nuts not to take you up on that," he said, his mouth creasing into a pleased smile.

She mentally blew out a breath, since it was highly likely that Jason could have been insulted about being bamboozled into dinner. Or he could have made plans for his Saturday night, and all of her cooking efforts would have been for naught. Even hermits had *some* friends.

Claire poured and handed Jason a glass of merlot while she put the finishing touches on the meal. After setting up Gina at the table in her booster seat, they all sat in the small dining room adjacent to the living room. She could count on one hand the number of times she'd used this dining set. She'd bought it when married to Charles, but since the divorce and moving into the bungalow, she'd hardly ever had guests.

Jason ate with gusto and paid numerous compliments about her cooking skills. It made her want to snap her fingers and dance in her chair. He also had a second glass of wine, and this time she joined him with her first. Surprisingly, he offered to do the dishes while she bathed Gina. All set for bed in her blanket sleeper, Gina hugged her new best friend goodnight. Though he'd been attentive enough to Gina during dinner, Claire saw Jason stiffen with the hug. And when Gina kissed his cheek, he flinched ever so slightly. Claire read Gina's favorite story in the bedroom to give Jason some time to himself, and the child fell immediately to sleep.

Claire stopped off in the bathroom to fluff her hair and put a bit more lip gloss on. Jason was a colleague. A friend, she reminded herself, but she thought about the goodlooking, suntanned man sitting in her living room and a shiver ran through her. Who was she kidding?

"I hope you don't mind, but I started a fire," he said, putting a second log in the fireplace when she returned.

Claire had only lived here for six months, and had rarely used the rugged rock fireplace. The golden glow and crackling fire made her already-small living room feel even cozier. He sat on the couch, and it occurred to her that it would be odd to sit in the chair all the way across the room, so she sat next to him. Then jumped back up.

"Oh, I should put on some decaf or tea to have with our pie."

He clasped her wrist and tugged her back down. "I need more time to digest that fantastic dinner first."

She landed a bit closer to him than she'd intended, but didn't move. The fire made her want to snuggle with someone. With Jason. Crazy thoughts. She'd blame the merlot.

Claire suspected Jason's gesture with the fire was a signal. Maybe he was reaching out to her. She protected herself with professionalism and went off on a safe and chatty tangent about all of the lame excuses their clinic patients had come up with for not returning their surveys. And if laughing proved he enjoyed listening to her, he must have. Good. They'd slipped back into a familiar level of comfort.

Jason told her about all of Gina's reactions to the animals at the zoo, though she sensed it was out of obligation. And he mentioned how she'd kept wishing her mommy were there. Claire had the urge to wake her daughter up and kiss her back to sleep. Jason must have noticed the depth of her love for her daughter, because when she ventured to look into his eyes they were steady and full of kindness, and they set off a warm implosion in her chest. She wasn't prepared for the reaction and pulled inward.

She noticed something else, too. His gaze had

clouded over with nostalgia, and it occurred to Claire how hard it must have been for him today, and she quickly regretted putting him through it.

"I think some coffee and pie are in order," Jason said, obviously sensing her shift in mood.

Hair had slipped across his forehead again, and the fire had warmed up the room enough for him to take off his sport jacket. She'd remembered his well-developed arms from the first day she'd met him, but tonight they looked particularly strong, and her resistance was suddenly weak. He followed her into the kitchen.

She'd made a huge mistake forcing him to spend the evening with her. He'd relaxed and she'd coiled tighter than a tangled Slinky. Her fumbling fingers proved he'd taken her out of her comfort zone. He seemed to watch her every move, and her cheeks heated up at the thought. Could she be anymore clumsy?

"I make a galley-chowder that will knock your socks off," he said with a broad smile. "That is if you like clams."

Grateful he'd tried to lighten the mood, she nodded. "Love chowder," she said, slicing the pie while the coffeemaker trickled steaming brown liquid into the glass pot.

"I'll have to invite you aboard sometime."

She almost cut a jagged line. Could she consider the invitation a date? Nah. Friends hung out on boats together. She handed him both pieces of pie, and followed behind with the mugs of coffee. They settled in front of the fireplace and sipped and ate and Jason made appreciative noises over the deliciousness of the apple pie. All of her efforts had paid off.

"This is the best crust I've ever had," he said. When he noticed she'd left a portion of hers on the plate he lifted his brows and reached for it. "You mind?" Without waiting for her answer, he popped it into his mouth.

It occurred to Claire that she'd never seen Jason act more naturally. He'd spent an afternoon with her daughter and survived. Now he seemed playful and content, probably from the carbohydrate overload, but still, it was progress.

She fell back into the cushions and put her feet up on the coffee table. "I'm so full I could pop." He watched her with amusement.

"I like that blouse," he said, totally taking her by surprise. "It suits you."

With cheeks on fire, as if she was a schoolgirl, she glanced at him, then at her hands. "Thanks."

Perhaps it was her sudden discomfort, but Jason touched her hand and stood. "I should probably be going," he said.

Her uneasiness had rubbed off on him. She regretted it. "Pipsqueak wore you out, eh?" she said, wanting to keep things light, and wishing she could rewind the moments that had changed his mood.

"Gina's a pistol. I get a real kick out of her," he said. "I'm kind of glad things worked out the way they did." He stopped mid-stride and looked deeply into her eyes. "There's something special about seeing the world through a kid's eyes. I've missed that."

Jason's nearness confused her. She hadn't

expected to turn into a shrinking violet under his scrutiny. Empathy had driven her to ask him to dinner. She'd accomplished her goal on that count, and he'd come out of his cave a little more tonight—an added benefit. She could pat herself on the back for making progress with him. But his penetrating gray eyes sent her straight back to last Friday night in his car. How many times had she relived those kisses this week?

Swept up by the moment, she reacted on impulse and kissed him goodnight. It was only a light peck on the lips, but more than a *friend* would give.

Jason seemed surprised at first, but he kissed her back, even put his hands on her waist to pull her closer. He tasted like nutmeg and sweetened apples. She wrapped her arms around his neck and soon they picked up where they'd left off before. There was no telling with Jason how long before he'd come to his senses and back out. So far so good. He'd found her tongue again and this time the sound effects were coming from *his* throat. She had to be delusional if she really thought she could keep theirs a friendship.

His hand discovered the skin beneath her blouse, and his warm touch sent tingles up her back. She kissed him frantically, afraid he'd change his mind again, and greed to touch him made her squeeze the muscles across his shoulders and arms. She traced light breathy kisses along his jaw and his grip tightened on her hip, the other hand edging closer to her bra.

He walked her backwards, and they managed to find the couch without breaking another of his deep kisses. He eased her against the sofa cushions with feathery lips down her neck. Her pulse flittered in her throat.

Jason pulled back to look at her, and she worried he would stop like he had before, but she saw the fire in his eyes. She hadn't imagined their *mutual* attraction after all. They'd been tugging and pulling on each other's libido since their first meeting, the day they'd yelled at each other. Maybe they could make this work. He was turned on and gorgeous and she made a snap decision to make love with him if he wanted her. From the hungry look in his eyes, he definitely wanted her. Now.

The fire crackled in the background and cast a bedroom glow over his face. His long fingers worked quickly to unbutton her blouse. He stopped briefly to look with obvious admiration at her lacy bra. Before she realized it, he'd undone the front clasp and released her. His hands caressed her breasts with near worshipful tenderness. His eyes briefly closed as his thumbs lightly swept across her nipples, and he swallowed before kissing the pebbled tips of first one and then the other. He wouldn't dare turn back now.

Claire savored the exquisite feel of his mouth on her breast. She couldn't believe how quickly she felt ready for him. She wanted to feel every part of him, and unbuttoned his shirt. They kissed again, ravenous kisses. She slid her hands under his shirt to pull it off, and was surprised to find smooth skin with little chest hair. She couldn't wait to see the rest of him.

Hot as the fire flaming across the room, she lifted his shirt above his head, and he eased her blouse and bra off her shoulders. Though nervous about what might happen, she gave herself to the moment and smiled, and he drew her flush to his chest. It felt like heaven to brush his skin with her breasts, to breathe his heated scent. He kissed her shoulder and toward the back of her neck, sending chills fanning across her skin. Every touch made her long for another. She tasted his faintly salty neck, slid her tongue along its surface, heard a sound deep in his throat and watched gooseflesh rise on his skin. She had him now, and savored every sensation awakening inside her. Tightening, heating, melting, pooling. She hadn't wanted to be with a man since her divorce. With only a few kisses, Jason had chased away every precaution.

She kissed his muscled chest, then lifted her chin to find his mouth again, but something had changed. The magnetic heat and longing she'd felt in the last moment had been tempered in the next. *Not again.* His tight embrace loosened, then went limp.

She wanted to scream, *no!* but kept kissing him, though he'd quit kissing back. Just like the other night. His warm lips had turned to rubber bands. She couldn't go through another rejection from him. Either he wanted her or he didn't.

He disengaged from her, rested his head on the couch and stared at the ceiling.

She'd sent mixed messages all night. She'd convinced herself she'd only wanted to share a friendly dinner with him, but whenever they got together things seemed to happen. He was obviously as confused as she was.

"Jason, we've got to talk about this."

He took a deep breath and shook his head. "I'm sorry."

"Is it me?"

"No," he answered in a flash. "It's me. It's them."

She knew he referred to his wife and daughter. "You can't go on punishing yourself for something you couldn't control."

"You're a beautiful woman, Claire." He made

a half-hearted reach for her fingers. "I'm just too messed up. Why screw you up, too?"

"Life doesn't come with a pain-free guarantee."

He glanced at her face, her breasts. "I still feel married. I'm sorry."

"It's been four years," she whispered.

As if paralyzed in the past, he didn't respond.

She buried her face in her hands. How could she argue with Jason's sense of faithfulness to his deceased wife? Wasn't that what every woman hoped for? For a man to be so devoted to her that he'd love her long after she'd died?

It occurred to Claire that it was a cruel wish for the loved one left behind. And, being on the other side of the scenario, she couldn't believe how wrong it felt. He'd punished himself, held back from living, and was willing to live half a life rather than risk being unfaithful to a memory. Or to feel again. Not that what they felt was love, but surely, with physical attraction such as theirs, the possibility of love could happen.

"I'll try to understand, but right now I feel as

if you're afraid to live," she said, "and you're using your deceased wife as an excuse."

His jaw tightened. He put his shirt back on. She remained topless on purpose. One of them needed to take a risk, and it was clear it wouldn't be Jason. His gaze drifted to her breasts again. She saw his hunger for her, but he wouldn't budge from his misguided martyr pedestal.

"I guess I'm just not ready to move on yet," he said, reaching for his jacket and heading toward the door. "I'm sorry."

Devastated, Claire chose not to show him out.

Sunday morning Jason took his smaller sailboat, the sloop he'd had since college, out to sea. He hadn't slept all night. He needed to get away. To go fast. He hoisted the mainsail and secured the halyard, then repeated the procedure with the jib. The wind was strong. He set up tight.

The sea would take his mind away from the vision of Claire, half nude and beautiful. At least that was his plan. So far the shifting of the azure waters had only reminded him more of her…in her gauzy blue blouse…and how he'd undressed her.

He scrubbed his face and reached for the tiller. There was no pretending. No going back. He and Claire had crossed a line. And he'd stumbled and fallen on his face.

He prepared to jibe and ducked as the sail swung from one side of the boat to the other. He'd thought he was the luckiest man alive to meet and fall in love with Jessica, but he'd lost her. Too soon. In the four years since she'd died, he'd had sexual urges but had never acted on them. They were the biological needs he'd endured as a widower, and had never been the result of an actual living breathing woman.

Until Claire.

Once he'd taken off her blouse he'd wanted nothing more than to be inside her. To know all of her. The thought made him reel. He couldn't forget Jessica. He was supposed to be with her.

Till death do us part…

Death had parted them. He'd lost his wife and daughter in the damn train wreck. Why couldn't he have died with them? The tears came, as they always did, and he bit back the salty taste. How was he supposed to move on?

The sun glared at him. He shut his eyes tight. Jessica's face materialized and drifted farther and farther away. He tried to will her back, but her image faded, and along with the next wave she disappeared as if sea mist. Then Claire's beaming face appeared and breezed over him like the wind.

After his crazy behavior with Claire he'd blown any chance of being with her. What woman would put up with his unpredictability?

The sloop had hit a dead sector and he trimmed the sails in tight, braced his feet on the deck and leaned out over the edge of the boat. He needed to change tack, head up toward the wind.

If only life was as easy as sailing.

Claire had survived a divorce. She would prevail over Jason's rejection, too. The man wasn't ready, and that was all there was to it. What made her think she was any more ready than him to get involved in a relationship? Hadn't her plan been to be his *friend*, not to jump all over his bones just because he was a good kisser and looked so damn sexy?

The man needed someone in his corner, not in his bed.

Time was the answer. The fact that they worked together would make things awkward for a while, but she was determined to keep her job and be whatever level of friend Jason would allow her to be. Her newly awakened fantasies of being with him sexually would just have to be put on hold.

Only one last question niggled in the back of her mind. Could she wait indefinitely?

Sunday afternoon she took Gina to visit Mrs. Densmore in the hospital. She still had some lingering muscle spasms and sympathetic nerve hyperactivity, and was being fed high caloric nutrition through a tube in her stomach, since she had a tracheotomy in her throat. Her rigid grin had disappeared, and it gave Claire hope all of her other symptoms would recede too.

Gina cried and didn't understand why Mrs. Densmore couldn't come home with them. And later, when she asked if she could see *Dock-to Wah-durs* and Claire said no, Gina got fussy and threw her cookie on the ground.

Monday morning in her office, Claire lost herself in paperwork and barely noticed Jason's footfalls in the hall. He paused at her door, freshly tanned, dressed to perfection in another perfectly tailored suit with a green shirt and complementary tie. At least his choice in clothes had brightened up.

The sight of him raised her nipples. So much for friendship.

"Good morning, Claire," he said in a deep and apologetic tone. At least he hadn't ignored her.

So he'd decided to take the safe route and pretend nothing passionate had happened between them, that they were business associates, nothing more. Be careful what you wish for. Hadn't she wanted to be his friend? If he needed a bland work existence, he could have it.

She glanced up from her desk. "Morning," she said, then went quickly went back to shuffling papers, determined not to look again until he'd left, though a trail of lost hope seemed to follow him down the hall. She wished things could be different, and gave a wry laugh, realizing that if wishes *could* make things different, Jason would still have a wife and child.

Where did that leave her?

By Thursday the civility was killing her, and she left her office door closed until after he'd arrived. She studied her scheduled appointments and noticed a patient she'd seen last week for stomach upset had been added on again today, and her symptoms had progressed to nausea, vomiting and problems with her vision. The new symptoms concerned Claire.

Instead of waiting until the afternoon to see the patient, Claire asked Gaby to have her come in this morning. She'd squeeze her in early between the other patients. By 10:00 a.m. Mrs. MacAfee had arrived. Claire had Gaby send the patient directly to their downstairs lab for stat blood tests.

She juggled two scheduled patients by sending one for X-rays and the other to Dr. Hanson's nurse for a blood gas test, then rushed Mrs. MacAfee into the newly vacated exam room.

One look at the poor woman and Claire knew she'd made the right decision.

Claire had discovered in her survey that this patient had been taking ginseng along with digoxin and due to the risk of toxicity had asked her to stop taking it immediately. She'd followed up with blood work, and fortunately the digoxin levels, though edging up to the high end, were within normal limits. Most importantly, her electrolytes had been in balance. With the new symptoms of nausea and vomiting, those lab findings could change today.

What concerned Claire the most was the patient's newest complaint of dimming vision.

"Tell me everything that has happened since last week," Claire said.

The woman recited a litany of problems, and Claire listened carefully for any clues.

"...and on top of that, I've been having such stomach problems, I think I may have ulcers," Mrs. MacAfee said.

"I can order a special upper endoscopy test for that, if you'd like."

The woman nodded enthusiastically. Claire made a note to write the referral to gastroenterology.

"You stopped the ginseng like we discussed, right?"

The woman nodded again, and Claire believed her. When she did her physical assessment, her blood pressure was within normal limits, though her pulse felt thready and fast.

"May I use the bathroom?" the woman asked, looking pale as if in need to vomit.

"Let me give you an emesis basin," Claire said.

"That's not what I need to do," the woman said.

Claire escorted her out the door and down the hall, just beyond Jason's office. Unfortunately, he was inside and seeing him after avoiding him all week made her stomach jump.

"When you're done go back to my exam room so my nurse can do an EKG."

Claire distracted herself by going over the patient's results, which had just been called up from the lab. Her eyes almost bugged out when she heard the digoxin level.

She rushed down the hall and tapped on the bathroom door. "Are you sure you stopped the ginseng, Mrs. MacAfee?" Nothing. Not a sound. "Mrs. MacAfee?" Claire jiggled the door handle and called her name out several more times.

Her nurse rushed over. "The skeleton key is on the door ledge," she said.

Claire felt around and found it, and opened the door to find Mrs. MacAfee passed out on the bathroom floor.

"Call a code assist," Claire said, checking the patient's carotid pulse. The woman was breathing and her pulse was present, though still thready. "I think she's dehydrated. Let's start an IV. But first let's get her on the gurney."

Jason appeared in the hall, pushing the emergency gurney toward them. "Let me help," he said.

"She's *dig* toxic and now she's passed out," Claire said, taking the woman's feet while Jason lifted under the patient's arms and hoisted her onto the gurney.

The next several minutes were a blur as they worked to start an IV and set up the EKG monitor. Mrs. MacAfee was slipping in and out of ventricular tachycardia. She needed to be in the E.R. stat.

"Call for an ambulance," Claire said to the nurse. Mrs. MacAfee's eyes fluttered; she fought to keep them open.

"Let's get some lidocaine on board," Jason said immediately after Claire placed the intravenous line.

As Claire opened the emergency cart, she added everything up in her head. The patient had all of the cardinal signs of digoxin toxicity: nausea, vomiting, anorexia, amblyopia. She'd need to be admitted to a monitored unit and receive antidigoxin antibody fragments, and to get her electrolytes back in balance. Claire shuddered, thinking about what might have happened if she hadn't brought the patient in this morning instead of waiting to see her in the afternoon.

But if Mrs. MacAfee had stopped the ginseng, what had made her digoxin levels continue to rise?

Jason stayed by Claire and the patient as the lidocaine drip helped stabilize the intermittent ventricular tachycardia on the monitor screen, and Mrs. MacAfee drifted in and out of consciousness. His presence brought her an added degree of confidence.

Once the ambulance arrived and the patient was safely on her way to the hospital, Claire took a deep breath and noticed Jason had put his hand on her shoulder. Instead of bringing comfort, the gesture made her tense up even more. She needed to get away from him, and made the excuse of calling the woman's husband.

An hour and a half later, eye to eye with Mr. MacAfee in the E.R. waiting room, Claire was grateful to deliver good news. His wife was responding to the treatment, and would be admitted to a monitor bed in the ICU. Once she'd calmed him down, she asked several of the questions floating through her mind.

"How long has she been complaining about stomach pain?"

"Two or three weeks," he said. "She'd started taking this special tea to help."

"Special tea?"

"A long time ago, a lady at the health food store told her that licorice tea was supposed to be good for stomach problems."

Off the top of her head, Claire had a vague memory about licorice being very helpful with soothing stomach pain and even treating ulcers, but why would the woman keep drinking it when she was getting progressively sicker? Buried in the myriad herbal treatments in her mind, a side-effect jumped out at Claire. Patients who used licorice and who were on digoxin were at risk for toxicity. No sooner had she weaned Mrs. MacAfee off one potentially dangerous drug/herb interaction with digoxin and ginseng, than the woman had replaced it with another—licorice.

After she informed the attending doctor at the hospital about the tea, and knowing Mrs. MacAfee was in good hands, she went back to the clinic. Bedraggled and stressed out, she nibbled at lunch at her desk, and took some extra red yam powder along with some anti-inflammatories to offset the ache she felt growing between her shoulders.

She heard a tapping at her door. It was Jason. Too tired to fight her feelings for him, she picked at her food and told him about discovering the licorice tea their patient had been taking unbeknownst to them.

"You can't know everything, Claire. You'll drive yourself nuts if you try," he said.

"Mrs. MacAfee jumped right out of the frying

pan and straight into the fire, and all she wanted to do was help herself feel better." Claire dug fingers into her hair and stared at her desk. "I don't think the survey was extensive enough. How do we get through to these people to check with us before adding any new herb to their regimen?"

"You said it was tea," he said, sounding far too level-headed. "How many people are going to think of tea as medicine? People on high blood pressure meds take over the counter cold medicine all the time, then they wonder why their blood pressure is sky-high afterwards. It's just human nature to try to take things into our own hands and fix it without bothering anyone else."

He looked far too sympathetic with his soft gray eyes as he walked around her desk, and sat on the edge. She tensed and sat back farther in her chair. If he touched her again, she might not have the strength to fend him off. And if he wasn't capable of reaching out emotionally, then she didn't want to start something that was bound to end badly. She'd be his friend and associate. That was her mantra and she was sticking to it.

"You can't catch everything, and you'll never be able to stop people from hurting themselves," he said softly.

How ironic the statement coming from Jason's beautifully formed lips, and she was on the verge of calling him out on it.

Someone tapped on the door. "Claire?" Her nurse. "Our first afternoon patient is here."

CHAPTER SEVEN

JASON unlocked his condo door. After the accident, he'd moved here from the luxurious family home set high on the hillside above Santa Barbara. He couldn't bear to live in the place filled with memories in every room. He'd been in shock at the time and could hardly function. Jon, Phil, and René had arranged everything: Found the condo; listed his house for sale; packed and moved him. In a daze, he'd followed along.

Even the spacious two-bedroom ocean-view condo felt too big for him to rattle around in. He'd lived here, if you could call it that, for the last three and a half years.

He tossed his jacket over the back of a chair, eased off his loafers, and padded across the hacienda-styled tiles to the kitchen. He poured some of the coffee left from the morning and warmed it in the microwave. As a bachelor, he could do that, not giving a damn how bitter it tasted. Heading straight to the terrace, he opened the French windows and sat at the glass and wrought iron table to sort through the mail he'd brought in.

His eyes were drawn to the coast and out to sea, the only constant thing in his life. How many times had he considered sailing off and never coming back?

Lately, the thought had less appeal. Since meeting Claire.

As it often did, his mind drifted to Claire. She'd been willing to give herself to him. The thought of her, topless and vulnerable, waiting for his touch, made him crinkle then wad up an advertising flyer.

I'm not ready to move on, he remembered telling her. And if by chance he were ready to get involved with her, was he ready to take the risk? Rationally, he knew Lupus wasn't deadly, that people lived with the autoimmune disease for years and years. But it affected the quality of life and, if not controlled, it could shorten hers. If he allowed himself to care for her, could he survive losing her? If a flare-up attacked an organ like her kidneys, she'd have to go to extreme treatment like chemotherapy to ward it off—a risky process. Was he ready for any possibility if he allowed himself to become involved with her?

Instead of only thinking of himself, he should consider her feelings. Was he a better man than her ex-husband?

He palmed his eye sockets and rubbed vigorously.

Would he look back at fifty and wonder why he'd squandered a chance at something real with a living breathing woman, when all he had left of Jessica was faded memories?

Opening up to Claire would be hard enough, but being around Gina made him ache so much for Hanna he could barely keep from tearing up at times. He remembered the wondrous look in his daughter's eyes whenever he'd taken her to the zoo, and he'd seen the exact same look on Gina's face the other day. His heart had twisted and cramped the entire afternoon Saturday.

It all felt too familiar. Claire and Gina. Jessica and Hanna. Maybe if Claire wasn't a parent. Maybe then easing back into a relationship wouldn't feel so daunting.

Right. And blink three times to make everything different and achieve world peace.

The child was just another excuse to stay living the life of a monk who preferred the sea to human beings.

After he'd finished his coffee he went back inside and, halfway down the hall, he stopped outside the guestroom door. He hadn't planned on coming here; he'd been heading for his bedroom. Yet here he was. All Jessica and Hanna's belongings that he couldn't bring himself to part with were stored inside. He thought of it as his torture room, the place he went to grieve and rent the air with painful moans and curses. Every leftover trace of their existence had been stored in this room. Things. Objects. Doodads. Jewelry. It was the room he entered when in a masochistic state, to sniff the few favorite dresses he'd kept of his wife's and mourn for their lost life and love. Again and again.

As if he thrived on punishment, a too-familiar routine, he turned the handle and went inside. The room was dim with drawn shades, and smelled stuffy. There was a stack of empty boxes Jon and René had left for him, and he'd kept promising to fill and give them away. He'd put it off for over three years.

He opened the closet door, where several dresses hung neatly in storage covers. He unzipped one and fingered the fabric, smooth and silky, tried to remember his wife wearing it, but couldn't. He sniffed the sleeve, but her scent had long vanished from the material.

A shelf of stuffed animals, everything from monkeys to cats to teddy bears, stared out at him from brightly colored faces and button eyes. He reached for a giraffe, one of Hanna's favorites. Its long neck had bent with time, and he thought how Gina might like it because of the giraffe they'd seen at the zoo, and set it aside.

He remembered how much he'd wanted to put his arms around Claire today when she'd been hurting, to offer her some support, but the threads from this tomb had held him back. He tilted his head at the notion that he'd never thought about anyone else before when he'd been in this shrine to his lost life. Yet Claire and her shining work ethic and heartfelt concern for one of the clinic patients had just woven its way into his thoughts.

He couldn't live out in the world if his heart was locked in here. The room closed tightly around him. The stale air made it difficult to breathe.

He'd begun to think about a better life. The kind of life he'd once shared with his wife and daughter, filled with laughter and love. And brightness. He glanced around the ever darkening room at the slowly disintegrating objects, and switched on the light. Jessica and Hanna were no more in this room than was Gemina the giraffe from the zoo.

Did he really want his memories to depend on disintegrating material and dust-covered toys?

No.

Jessica and Hanna would remain forever in his heart, but not here.

The irony hadn't gone unnoticed. He'd mentally chastised Claire's husband for walking away from a living, breathing, wonderful woman, and here he was doing the exact same thing by shutting up his heart in this stagnant room and keeping her at a distance.

Jason looked over his shoulder at the boxes and back at the objects that could never bring his wife and daughter back, and scooped up most of the toys, then deposited them into the nearest box. Next he gathered Jessica's shoes, her clothes and almost all of her jewelry. An hour later, feeling an odd burden lift from his shoulders, he placed a call to the local rescue mission to arrange for them to pick up everything but one small box.

Thursday evening, after making a brief hospital visit to Mrs. Densmore, who remained stable,

Claire rushed to the babysitter's to pick up Gina. Her daughter's bright eyes and beaming smile made up for all the frustration and self-doubt she'd harbored from the day. They hugged and giggled and Gina told her all about her adventures with her new "bestest" friend, Emily.

Their daily routine of dinner, bath, reading a book, sometimes a second book, and bedtime, helped distract her thoughts from Jason. He'd been on her mind a lot all week. It was just her luck to accidentally find an intelligent, appealing and sexy man, only to discover he was incapable of having a relationship.

OK, she got the point. She'd finally learned her lesson about closed off men. They couldn't be changed and they only brought heartache. She wasn't going to beat her head against any walls on Jason's behalf. She'd done her share of wishing things could be different with her ex-husband, and it had only proved one thing. Things didn't change. People didn't change.

The next time she let herself get involved with a man, it would be with a guy who was crazy about her, an open and caring guy whose only desire was to make her happy.

Didn't she deserve it? And, more importantly, did that guy exist?

Friday morning, Claire saw a routine ear infection on the verge of perforating in a six-year-old boy, and prescribed the pink bubblegum-flavored medicine to ensure he'd take all of it as indicated. By late that afternoon she got word that the child was in the E.R. with anaphylaxis. She wanted to cry. The mother had assured her the child didn't have any allergies to medicine, yet he'd had a life-threatening reaction to what should have been a harmless and helpful antibiotic.

What else could go wrong?

She threw a book across the room in frustration, then flinched when it inadvertently shattered a vase. She grimaced, and rushed over to pick up the glass.

"Damn, damn, damn," she grumbled.

"What's going on?" Jason had caught her at her worst. Again.

"I seem to have a knack for almost killing our

patients!" The events and surprising outcomes of the last couple of days had made her lose confidence. A sudden whirlwind of emotions ranging from anger to fear took hold and made her eyes sting, and soon she couldn't control the release of tears. Why did Jason have to see her crumbling in defeat like this?

He rushed toward her, concern furrowing his brows. "Don't touch the glass, you'll cut yourself."

"It would serve me right," she said, sounding petulant.

"I'll call the janitor to clean this up, but first you have to tell me what's wrong," he said, and placed his hands on her shoulders to steer her back to her desk chair. There it was, the little surface explosion on her skin whenever he touched her, even now.

"I ordered antibiotics for a peds patient who turned out to be allergic."

"It happens. We can't predict how our patients are going to react."

He handed her a tissue, called Gaby to alert

Mr. Hovanissian about the problem, then placed his hands back on her neck and started a gentle rolling massage. Unlike her patient, she *could* predict how she was going to react.

"Please don't touch me," she whispered.

He immediately backed off. "I didn't mean to upset you, Claire. I'm not an acupressure expert, but I thought a neck massage might help you relax."

She wanted to be snide and say, *and just when I start to like it you'll stop,* but swallowed instead.

"You're as tightly strung as one of the jam cleats on my boat."

"I don't have a clue what that is," she said.

"Sounds like reason enough to bring you out on the boat sometime. Trust me, it's tight. Tight enough to snap. I'd be remiss if I let that happen to you."

Claire heard both concern and sincerity in his tone.

"Look, you've had a tough week, and I hate to see you like this," he said as he rubbed his hands together. "They're nice and warm. Why don't you give it a try?" His silver eyes almost twinkled with goodwill.

She remembered his warm hands on her body and how incredibly good they'd felt.

Whether poor judgment or unadulterated weakness, she swiveled in her chair so he could rub her neck. At first she tensed more, but realizing how she'd let her job affect her body, which could set off her Lupus, she allowed Jason to continue. He had magic fingers, and she let him knead and stroke her aching neck and shoulder muscles. The raised hairs on her skin, and the accompanying goose bumps, would have to be dismissed as a side-effect of stress relief, nothing more. She hoped he'd buy that lame excuse.

Claire was grateful when the janitor appeared and Jason removed his soothing hands. He might not want to have a relationship with her, and she'd vowed for sanity's sake to be nothing more than a friend, but his mere touch had made her damp and wishing she had a pullout bed in her office. So much for her resolve.

One more thought occurred to her as Mr. Hovanissian swept up the shards of glass. Now that she'd given up on Jason Rogers, he seemed to be the one person at her side at the first sign of a crisis.

That evening at home, Claire had changed into her sweats to do laundry when she heard a tapping on her door.

It was Jason, with a sheepish look on his face. He nodded, rather than say hello.

Unsure of what else to do, Claire invited him in.

From behind his back he pulled a huge-eyed, gangling giraffe with a bent neck.

"What's this?"

"I thought Gina might like to have it."

"That's very sweet, but she's already asleep. I think you should wait and give it to her yourself. She'd really like that."

"Is that an invitation to stay the night?"

Claire went still.

"That was a joke, Claire." He nodded again, and seemed to hesitate about leaving. "I've been doing some house cleaning," he said. "That belonged to my daughter."

The fact he'd been clearing out his daughter's belongings sent a clear message: he was trying and, as a friend, she needed to be supportive of his efforts. Trying? Hell, his efforts were monumental.

Her thoughts felt so clinical, yet she had to protect herself. A knot bunched in her chest. The gesture of giving Gina one of Hanna's stuffed toys was beyond kind. It made her want to cry. The man had a good heart. A wounded and healing heart. He just wasn't sure how to use it anymore.

And he had a body which would waste away without benefit of touch or love because he couldn't let go of his lost family. She gazed at him standing there looking gorgeous as always. He'd even attempted a dorky joke about staying the night. That was definitely progress on the Jason Rogers front.

"Come in and sit for a while," she said. "Tell me about this." She held up the giraffe and he followed her to the living room, though neither of them sat.

"Last night, I cleared out an entire room of 'things' that belonged to Jessica and Hanna. I'd been hoarding them, as if I could scrape off their DNA and make them come back to life." She could see the familiar pain in his eyes, but he communicated something else, too. Something had definitely changed. Maybe he'd had some kind of breakthrough. Her whirling thoughts kept her from uttering a sound.

"Someone at the rescue mission is going to get a whole new wardrobe," he said, making a rueful smile. "Even if some of the clothes are out of date."

Claire had been wallowing in guilt and self-doubt over Mrs. MacAfee's problem, and for sending a child into anaphylaxis. She'd been self-centered. This beat-up giraffe quickly reminded her again of the oppressive grief Jason must have had to endure every day of his life for the past four years. It made her problems seem infinitesimal. Being reminded again of his devastating loss made her want to weep.

It made her want to love him.

She broke free from the self-imposed caution and took two long strides to meet him. Her hands cupped his face, forced him to look into her eyes. She prided herself on reading people, and it was pain and hope she saw in his gaze. Overwhelmed by the sacredness of his admission, and the dusty and goofy-looking stuffed toy he offered, she longed to ease his pain. An optimistic rise in her heart caused her to throw away all caution and concern, and she covered his face with kisses. Instead of worrying about herself, she'd think only of him.

And, without hesitation, he kissed her back.

Jason caught her lips with his own and feathered kisses at each corner. Happy kisses. Smiling kisses. Laughter bubbled up between them, then disappeared as her hands wrapped around his neck and his arms stretched around her back.

They kissed, as they always had, with passion

and lust, and when the heat had turned up to the point of no return, and Jason gave no sign of quitting before the fun began, she walked him down the hall to her bedroom.

Jason found Claire's bedroom to be reflective of her: uncluttered, bright and colorful. Daffodil-yellow walls, a large dark wood bed frame with a padded leather headboard. Extra pillows encased in patterned and solid-colored shams to complement the muted green duvet. One lone dresser across the room matched the bed, and a full length oval-shaped mirror on a stand took up residence in the other corner.

He glanced at Claire; color was rising to her cheeks. He'd done that to her—his kisses, his craving to be inside her; his single-minded desire to finally break out of his self-imposed celibacy.

He wanted nothing more than to express with his body how he felt about Claire. Words couldn't do justice to the cresting, powerful feelings rolling through him. He pulled her sweatshirt over her head, happy to find she wore nothing beneath it.

His hands roamed across the soft tissue of her warm breasts, and quickly found the silken rosy skin around her nipples. They tightened from his touch, and teased him to take them into his mouth. When he did, her encouraging murmurs and invitations made him rock-hard.

She stripped off his shirt, and soon they were both naked, his sailor's tan a contrast to her creamy tones. She smiled at him with blazing eyes, and he took her mouth with his, holding her flush to his body. Her long and slender legs allowed their stomachs to touch, sending a shockwave of tingles across his skin, and his erection grew firmer.

He smoothed his hands across her back and along the curve of her hips, then pulled her closer. She felt like heaven and smelled like a tropical garden. They stood undulating body to body through several more penetrating kisses, until he couldn't take another second standing up.

He lifted Claire, placed her on the bed and lay down beside her. Her arms quickly wrapped him close, and their kissing started all over again. His hand traced along her flat stomach and found the light patch of hair he'd only glimpsed before. He kissed her mouth, searched for and found the dampened smooth skin between her legs, and the area that made her moan when his finger slid over it. He lingered there and, with their lips and tongues penetrating each other's mouths, his fingers mimicked the motion below.

She rocked against him, quickening his touch, and wrapped her leg around his hip, pressing the tip of his erection to her thigh, sending a shock wave through his groin. While his excitement flourished, he brought her to quick release.

He watched her; his own nerve endings vibrated and tingled as he strained with longing. Sensations from every part of his body converged in a powerful force until he had to be inside her. It had been four years since he'd made love; he couldn't wait one more second. He rolled her to her back and parted her legs, pressing hard and long at her entrance.

Claire's hands held tight on his hips, urging

him inside. The inviting expression on her face from earlier had changed to one of pure need.

Crazy with desire, he looked into her fiery eyes. Her surprisingly strong hands urged him deeper, and he didn't put up a fight. His response was no longer under his control. He slipped inside her luscious warmth and thought only of Claire as they rocked together toward satisfaction. Forgotten sensations and her exquisite body lured him deeper, straining for relief.

She rolled on top and held his shoulders as their hips lifted and rolled like the sea. The vision of her straddling him nearly sent him over the edge much sooner than he wanted. But she was all powerful, and her controlled rhythm pushed his desire to the brink. He flipped her onto her back and drove deeper inside, again and again, and she rose and spasmed around him, driving out the last of his resistance.

Thinking only of Claire, the here and now, he thrust against her perfect fit, until he caught up with her and they came together. His release was the most intense since he'd been a randy teenager. It racked throughout his body and seemed to last forever. He caught his breath and watched while her eyes fluttered and her face strained against the same consuming sensations he felt rolling through his body.

After years of deep-seated pain, he'd finally plunged into new territory and had rediscovered long forgotten feelings. She'd given him profound pleasure and, from the look of Claire's euphoric smile, he'd done the same for her.

Before he could think another thought, Claire pulled him toward her soft and inviting body, and they lay entwined in a state of bliss in the kind and welcoming light of her bedroom.

CHAPTER EIGHT

"DOCK-TO WAH-DURS!"

The next morning, Claire's eyes popped open to find Gina jumping on the bed in her powder-puff-pink sleeper. She'd meant to wake Jason up early before Gina got up, and to have it appear as if he'd shown up for breakfast, but they'd made love throughout the night and finally, just before dawn, collapsed in deep sleep.

Their hunger for each other had been equal and nearly insatiable. She'd never been pushed to such limits with her husband. Jason had spent four years living as if a monk, and when he'd finally broken through his unnatural vigil, his basic need had been astounding.

Not having ever been in this situation since her divorce, Claire scrambled to think of something to say to Gina.

Jason rose up on his elbows, dark brown hair draped across his forehead. "Hey, squirt, who told you to wake us up?"

"Why you here?" Gina asked.

He glanced at Claire, who wanted to hide under the sheets. "Um, he brought you a present." *He had a mind-blowing surprise for Mommy, too!*

"Where is it?" Gina, who had stopped long enough to ask her question, jumped up and down again. Fortunately, her curiosity about her mother's bed partner had been overshadowed by the present, though in the future she vowed to be much more discreet.

Claire sent Gina off to the living room to retrieve the giraffe from the couch, then glanced at Jason. "What should we do?"

He pecked her on the lips, threw back the covers and slid into his jeans before Gina could find him in all his gorgeous male glory. "I'll make breakfast. That's what we'll do."

Gina came galloping down the hall. "It's Gemina! It's Gemina!"

"That's right, squirt, it's Gemina," he said.

After a surprisingly relaxed morning together, Jason left to make his hospital rounds with a promise to call Claire later. Somewhere after the coffee and before the French toast, she felt a subtle shift in his demeanor, but couldn't quite pinpoint what had occurred. She hoped he didn't regret what they'd done. He kissed her goodbye, but Gina giggled and commented, "You kissing, Mommy," and Jason cut the cool kiss short.

Claire went about her usual Saturday chores, though nothing was remotely the same from the last time she'd cleaned her house. Last weekend she'd been confused and frustrated by Jason's unpredictable behavior, and this weekend he'd left her both aroused and sated, happy and concerned. Why did life have to be so confusing?

Her body hadn't hummed this much since

puberty, and she'd risked total openness with Jason last night. If he rejected her now, it might tear her to the core, but she'd survive. Because she'd held something back.

Her heart.

She had to.

Claire was in charge of her feelings and she'd guard them, because of Gina. Her baby had already gotten attached to "Dock-to Wah-durs" and Claire couldn't bear the thought of Gina getting her heart broken.

Driving home to change his clothes before checking in on his list of hospitalized patients, Jason got hit by a tailwind. He'd broken through a huge barrier with Claire, and the results had been amazing. Claire was everything in a lover he'd missed. The long legs, high small breasts, and curves in all the right places were definitely a plus, but something else made the difference when they'd made love. She was open, responsive, and assertive. Just thinking about her made his body react.

He felt alive today. He'd come out of his coma. The sensations that had rippled through him last night had cleared his head. Rippled? More like white water rafting, he thought with another grin erupting.

The beach looked whiter, the water clearer, and the sky endlessly blue. And, for someone who'd never given a damn about palm trees, today, their existence added the perfect touch to his picturesque city. Was this what he'd been missing out on? He continued to grin and thought about Claire in several appealing positions, and almost turned his car around.

Yet something else held him back, and it came in a tiny pink package. The breakfast scene in the kitchen had felt too much like old times with his family. He'd managed to separate Claire from Jessica—they were very different in stature, appearance, personality, demeanor, well, just about everything. But each glance at Gina reminded him of Hanna and the injustice of her life being stolen. Gina's big blue eyes, and the innocence they reflected, tore at his heart and kept the old wounds raw and jagged. She was easy enough to be around, with a good disposition in general, but he had found himself recoiling from her as the morning had gone on. He couldn't help it.

As he drove past the harbor, Jason spotted his boat down the dock. "I can't quit thinking about Hanna when I'm around Gina," he muttered as he pushed the gas for a green light.

He needed to think of a way for him and Claire to be together all by themselves. And that realization made him aware of an old and constant companion—guilt.

That evening, Jason showed up at Claire's house with Chinese takeout, and a kids' DVD for Gina. After eating dinner, Claire and Jason snuggled and kissed while Gina sat rapt, watching *Pinocchio*.

As the hour drew on, Claire expected Jason to stay and make love to her again. Instead, he got up to leave. "I've got an early day sailing tomorrow. Hey, would you like to come out with me?"

She knew his passion for sailing. She also knew the sun was deadly for her Lupus. And what about Gina? "Too much sun can set off a flare."

He anchored his hand under her chin and drew her close enough to kiss. After a slow, warm and teasing taste of what he could do to her, he broke it off. "That's why they make broad-brimmed hats and thirty block sunscreen."

She fought off her schoolgirlish reaction to him. They'd explored every part of each other last night; what was there to feel shy about? "You've got a point, but maybe another time? I don't have anyone to watch Gina tomorrow." She didn't want to hit him over the head with it, but she definitely wanted to give him a hint about including her daughter, who'd never been sailing, either.

"Next weekend. Just you and me." He reached for her hands. "Come away with me." He lifted a brow and the tempting glint in his eyes seemed irresistible.

She brushed away the hair from across his brow and the plethora of thoughts and questions racing through her mind: Do I dare let go and run with this man? Is it a mistake to get involved with my boss? Has he really had a breakthrough? Will he pull back again? What about Gina? "OK."

He kissed her again, slower this time. They folded into each other and shared lingering, inviting kisses. He breathed deep and glanced toward her bedroom. She smiled and rested her forehead to his, clearly on the same wavelength.

"I'd better go," he whispered.

Surprised by the contradiction, she took a chance. "You can stay if you want to."

"You know I do, but…" he said, avoiding her eyes.

She could feel him retreating. She tried to put herself in his position. It had been four years since he'd lost everything. He was finally venturing back into life. Another night of passionate lovemaking might be too overwhelming. She'd let him define his own re-entry.

"I've got a lot of stuff to do tomorrow," he said.

"I understand," she said, her emotions contradicting her words. The best she could do was *try* to understand.

One step forward, two steps back, Jason thought as he drove up the coast past the small college and toward home. He could have been making love to Claire right this minute, but he'd taken the coward's route and left. He didn't want her to think he was using her, and he'd been out of the loop for so long, he hadn't a clue what a guy did in a situation like this. If he went with his feelings he'd be making love to Claire right now, but he'd put on the brakes. Something told him to slow down.

With Claire, he wouldn't just be dating her, he'd be involved with Gina, too. He'd made it over one hurdle, only to stumble on the next. Claire was a package deal, and though her daughter was as cute as a button, the double whammy of moving beyond being a devout widower into a relationship, *and* having to be a father of sorts, too…well, it boggled his mind and messed with his mojo.

He'd been in a pleasant light state of sleep that morning, slowly feeling his body come alive—in one part in particular—when the earthquake named Gina had rocked and rolled into the bedroom. He'd been thinking about making love to Claire again, but Gina had changed his plans. Fortunately, they'd made love a couple of times last night. He may have been out of practice but, with Claire's amazing help, he'd quickly gotten into the swing of things. And they'd been damn good together. A satisfied smile stretched across his face, then quickly faded.

Gina popped into his thoughts again. The little one had a father. He wouldn't be stepping into anyone's shoes. It was Hanna, his precious girl, who tugged at his memory and gazed at him with her huge brown eyes. He'd finally made peace with Jessica and his desire for Claire, but who would have guessed that losing his child would be the hardest thing to let go of?

Don't forget me, Daddy.

He'd never forget her.

Never.

* * *

Monday at work, Claire worried she and Jason were a bit obvious when they grinned at each other like fools, and when she turned four shades of red, while he went directly into bedroom eyes mode right in front of Gaby. But it was the first time they'd seen each other since Saturday, and they'd happened to meet up at the receptionist's desk. How could one day away from each other seem like a week?

He'd called her Sunday night when he'd arrived home from sailing. After they'd chatted for a while, something that seemed effortless and as if he'd been gone for weeks with so much to catch up on, they'd made plans to eat lunch together. And, if it was another beautiful spring day, they'd eat under the ash tree. She'd fixed her special chicken salad with sliced grapes, celery, walnuts and cinnamon, and had brought chocolate chip cookies because she'd remembered they were his favorite.

Later that day all the nurses, even René, made a double take out the kitchen window as she and Jason sat on the bench under the tree, laughing and eating together.

The late spring weather was inviting and warm enough for Claire to leave her lab coat in her office. She wore a fuchsia-colored top and, around her neck, several strings of tiny beads in various shades of purple. She'd applied vanilla and spice body lotion, and had used the curling iron on her hair. He'd made her feel pretty again, not like the unattractive, chronically ill woman her husband had seen. She wanted to impress Jason, to keep him looking at her as if she were the prettiest girl in the room and, judging by Jason's continuous enamored gaze as they ate, she'd achieved her goal.

Nibbling on a walnut, she smiled a Mona Lisa smile and thought about her new guy and her great job, and how life was definitely looking up.

"Do you remember the first week you started here?" he asked.

Quickly swimming out of her thoughts, she nodded. "Of course."

"The day you ate your lunch out here and thought a bee had flown into your hair?"

She stopped mid-chew. He'd given her a bee-keeper's hat after that day. It was the first sign she'd had that the guy had a sense of humor, but his gesture had rankled her and made her feel embarrassed.

There was an impish glint in his gaze. "I saw the whole thing," he said, a smile tickling at one edge of his mouth, soon spreading to the other side.

She cuffed him on the arm as her face grew hot. "How embarrassing. Why do you have to bring it up again?"

"I thought it was cute. Enchanting. I knew you'd be someone special to me right then, because you could make me laugh, make me feel things, but I kept myself in denial for as long as I could."

Were these wonderful confessions coming from the closed off man she knew Jason Rogers to be? Touched by his openness, she squeezed his arm. She wanted to blurt out her "special" feelings for him, too, but being at work and realizing people might be watching, and so early in the relationship, she opted to keep it light.

And to add a little spice. "You weren't exactly the easiest man to work with, you know," she said.

"And you came off a little ditzy." He grinned and popped a whole cookie into his mouth.

Claire tried to be insulted, but Jason's cockeyed and charming expression defused her reaction. She liked the new swagger to his style. It turned her on.

After he'd swallowed, he glanced over his shoulder toward the kitchen window, where Gaby and the nurses had huddled around the sink as if washing dishes, a poor excuse to spy on them. He turned back to Claire and leaned forward. "Why don't we really give them something to talk about?"

He took her by the hand and led her around the other side of the enormous tree trunk and, once safely out of their view, he did what she'd been hoping he'd do ever since she'd seen him that morning. He kissed her.

* * *

The week at the clinic sped by with manageable patients, no medical surprises, and a kindling heat in Claire's belly to make love with Jason again. He'd apparently wanted to make sure she'd go sailing with him by holding off on getting skin to skin until the weekend. With her awakened physical desire for Jason, against her better judgment, she agreed to try the wide-brimmed hat, long sleeves and sunscreen method for dealing with the sun on his sailboat. She also hoped for an overcast sky.

Thursday afternoon, Claire got word that Mrs. Densmore was being discharged from the hospital. She'd have a home health aid around the clock the first few days, and nurses visiting a couple of times a week, but Claire felt compelled to accompany her home and make sure everything was in proper order.

When she arrived at the hospital ward, she came prepared to be sent to the business office and, with her credit card in hand, hoping she'd have enough to pay the balance for whatever had accrued, she marched down the hall.

"She's all set to go," the nurse in charge of Mrs Densmore said.

"Don't I need to sign my life away?" Claire asked.

The seasoned nurse studied the discharge papers and raised a graying brow. "Everything's been taken care of by Dr. Rogers."

Claire paused. As she accompanied the nurses' aide rolling her landlady out to the car, she thought about Jason and how he'd paid the medical bills. The thought edged her one step closer to falling in love with him.

Charles had agreed to take Gina for the weekend, and, after dropping her daughter off Friday evening, Claire nervously finished packing her bags as Jason knocked at her door.

"We'll eat and sleep on board tonight," he said, "then tomorrow after dawn we'll set sail." He brushed her lips in greeting. "You taste great." He kissed her again, and every spark imaginable jumped between them. "And you feel even better."

Relieved that he hadn't forgotten how great they were together, a laugh tumbled from her chest. "This has been the second longest week of my life."

"And what would be the first?"

"My first week at the clinic, having to face the world's biggest grump everyday." She smiled playfully.

"Don't have a clue who you're talking about," he said, and made a sweeping glance from her head to toes, as though conjuring up a great idea.

Before she knew it, they'd forgotten all about dinner and had landed back in her bed for a send-off session of lovemaking.

Could life get any sweeter?

Hours later, in the cabin below deck, Jason wrapped his arm around Claire as they snuggled together in the cozy bunk bed. The undulations of the harbor water gently rocked them toward sleep. Claire was the only other woman he'd ever brought here. He glanced out the cabin porthole and into the clear night sky to catch a glimpse of the waxing gibbous moon. It glistened on the water, and Jason knew in his gut he'd done the right thing by asking her to come with him.

"I've missed this." He hadn't meant to say it aloud, but the words had popped out regardless.

Claire furrowed her brow, as if the phrase wasn't what she'd hoped to hear.

Earlier he'd given her a tour of the narrow chambers he called home while at sea. He'd replaced the cabin sole with teak wood for added warmth the summer before the train wreck. The mahogany cabinets and brass fixtures were original and gave the cabin its authentic nautical feel. The galley, complete with stainless steel sinks and stove, was well planned without an inch of wasted space. Every item was secured in place. The leather upholstered booth with thickly varnished wood table could easily seat four for meals. He proudly kept his boat in shipshape by spending most weekends either cleaning or sailing, as an excuse to avoid the rest of his life.

It had made him smile when he saw the genuine awe and excitement on Claire's face as she'd explored the smaller cabin and head. He'd always prided himself on being completely contained on *Hanna's Haven*, even after his world had come to an end.

And yes, he'd missed sharing it with someone. He was glad it was Claire.

Jason studied her face by the moonlight. She had slipped off to sleep. Her lashes were long, and the tiny tension lines between her brows that always seemed to be there at work, had disappeared. He dipped his head and gently kissed her forehead, then held her a little closer.

The next morning he gave Claire a short lesson on what she could do to help him and, being a quick study, she caught right on. They set sail on a glassy-smooth sea. She gave no sign of being seasick after sleeping on the boat, but he still suggested she take a pill to fight off any potential nausea from rough patches at sea.

The success of their trip would depend on an invisible and ever varying force—the wind. And the success of their relationship would depend on another invisible force—his desire to finally break free and move on in his life. Was he there yet? He had a feeling this weekend would give him the answer.

Claire wore loose white pants and a bright yellow zip-neck, long-sleeved crew shirt with one of his old sailing jackets as she re-emerged from the galley Saturday morning. She brought two seaworthy mugs of coffee with her. The crisp morning air bit through his windbreaker and had quickly woken him up. But not until Claire had delivered his coffee and slipped under his free arm, as he manned the tiller, did he feel alive. He smiled as her hair flapped beneath her baseball cap with the extra-wide brim. It hid her eyes, and he wanted to take it off so he could see them, but knew it protected her from the sun's harmful rays.

She was beautiful, and tightened the sinews of his chest just by gazing into his eyes and dropping sweet, reassuring kisses on his lips. Each one made him eager for another. The day was bright and the sea ebbed and flowed beneath the boat. It was a fine day for sailing.

"Do you have your sunscreen on?"

"Aye, aye, Captain," she said.

Just before noon he navigated through an amazing section of ocean, the dolphin feeding grounds. Hundreds of the mammals leapt and frolicked around their boat. Pods had joined together in aggregates to fish and play, and several of them seemed to chase the sailboat. Their powerful flukes propelled them through the tealblue water in a most entertaining way. Claire laughed and gasped at their antics, and exclaimed she'd never seen anything like it in her life, and Jason played along, challenging the dolphins to try to catch him. They shared a smile followed by a kiss, and Jason thought the day was close to perfect.

By early afternoon they'd reached Anacappa Island off the Ventura coast, and found a quiet cove in which to anchor. Claire quickly disappeared into the galley to make lunch while Jason tended the sails. When he'd just about finished, Claire called out his name.

"Jason? Lunch is ready!"

A minute later, he hustled downstairs to find her resplendent and waiting for him…wearing nothing but a huge grin.

"Coffee, tea or me?" she said.

Amazed by her radical surprise, he couldn't get undressed fast enough.

Claire didn't know where this crazy idea had come from. It seemed completely out of character for her, but with Jason it felt astoundingly right. Maybe it was the constant roll of the ocean, or Jason looking super-masculine manning the schooner. Or the fact that she wanted to do something to blow his mind, so he'd never forget the day he'd taken Claire Albright to sea. Whatever the reason, she'd taken a deep breath and stripped down and had been rewarded by an ultra-appreciative stare when he'd entered the galley.

Jason disrobed fast as a squall, rushed to her and dove into her neck with kisses as one hand weaved into her hair and the other located her breast. They kissed eagerly and wantonly, and her hands roamed over every bit of his flesh she could find. She'd been ready for him before he'd even found her naked, and with little effort he'd already grown hard.

Before she realized it, he'd lifted her hips and sat her on a counter, the perfect height for him to press into her, which he did quickly and with vigor. The rush of hot sensations made her cry out.

"Did I hurt you?" He stopped abruptly.

"No," she said breathlessly. She kissed him firmly as she wrapped her legs around his waist so he could deepen the penetration and soothe her edging desire.

He used the counter as leverage and dove into her time and time again. "I think I'm falling for you," he whispered over her ear, taking her totally by surprise.

She wanted to say something back to him, searched for the words, but he'd taken control of her body and she couldn't form a single thought, let alone a sentence. Both heat and chills fanned across her skin. Every hair seemed to stand on end. His unyielding thrusts found their mark, teasing and tightening her insides into frenzy as her mind whirled with his confession. He was falling for her.

Her nipples ached with pleasure that coiled through her belly. She came quickly with a consuming shudder and wave after wave of tingles under her skin.

She'd barely recovered when he thickened and pulsed inside her with several more lunges. The building wave started again, and she felt as if she were spiraling through the air until she came undone a second time, matching his powerful release.

They held on to each other as if they'd disappear once they let go. He may have stunned her silent with both his actions and words, but in her heart she'd already fallen for him. Could love be next?

After Jason made a makeshift canopy on deck for Claire, she snuggled beneath and watched him do a little fishing. If he got lucky, he might catch their main course for dinner. Or so he'd promised. The seasick pill she'd taken earlier in the day had made her drowsy, and she floated off to sleep without a care in the world.

Later, heat and a trickle of sweat woke her up. She checked her watch. It was four o'clock, the sun had shifted and was still bright and shining off the water, right into her eyes. She searched for Jason on deck, but he was nowhere around.

She shook her head to help wake up, and scooted out of the sun's direct path.

Jason appeared with a large iced tea, and she greedily reached for it as the combination of sun and medicine had made her thirsty.

"On the other side of Santa Cruz Island—" he pointed to another island out further "—there's a place called Potato Bay. It's well protected from the sea, and I thought we'd sail over there and anchor for the night. In the morning we can do some hiking before we head home."

"That sounds wonderful. Count me in, Captain."

He kissed her, then put her to work on the jib while he lifted anchor and manned the mainsail. He sailed into the constant wind and made good time. They found the bright blue horseshoe-shaped bay surrounded by high jagged cliffs, and she saw hikers along the edges waving down at them and she waved back. Two other boats had moored across the way. Jason anchored the boat and prepared dinner before sunset.

Opting to eat outside, they sat on the smooth varnished wood of the deck and had a picnic. Jason poured a rich burgundy wine and, because he hadn't been successful fishing, they broke off pieces of baguette and ate assorted cold cuts and cheeses along with grapes, nuts and orange wedges.

With a light breeze lifting her hair, Claire couldn't remember when she'd felt more alive. Jason had shown her a whole new world at sea and she liked it, thought she could grow to love it. And him. She knew about his haunting battle with his lost family, and the thought of being treated differently because of it, or forever held at a distance, worried her. Would she have enough patience to give him time to heal? It had already been four years.

Earlier Jason had said, "I think I'm falling for you." The kind of phrase a woman longed to hear from the right guy. A stepping stone toward the promise of love. Yet his comment felt more like a general statement that had slipped out of his mouth in the heat of passion, and she'd just happened to be in on it. He'd taken her by total surprise.

He'd invited her into his world, but he'd never discussed anything personal with her, other than telling her about the train wreck. And he'd never mentioned it since.

She had no idea how he felt about getting involved with a woman with a chronic illness. Would he get bored with her need to rest more than the average woman, as Charles had? Could he understand that relapses would happen, no matter how diligent she was with her medicine and holistic remedies? Charles never had. Would he hold her responsible for any setbacks, as her ex-husband had?

Each step closer to Jason forced so many more questions.

Claire came out of her thoughts and scratched her neck in answer to a blossoming itch. It dawned on her that her face felt warm and tight. She'd slipped up by falling asleep and getting exposed to the sun; now she feared she'd set off a Lupus rash.

"What's the matter?" Jason asked.

She touched her face. His eyes widened. He put down his wine and came close enough to examine her.

"You're pink, looks like sunburn across your nose and cheeks."

"I'd better double up on my NSAIDS. I don't want to wind up on steroids unless I have to."

Jason jumped up. "I've got some ibuprofen in the cabin. Let me get them for you."

"Could you bring up my purse? I've got some

wild yam and licorice extract I should probably take, too."

Despite doing her best to avoid the sun on the sailboat, she'd still gotten a sun rash. Would she have to paint her face in zinc oxide and look like a ghost in order to sail with him? Sailing was Jason's true passion in life, and she'd already flunked the test at being a part of it. What did that say for the odds of them being together?

He brought her some water and a couple of anti-inflammatories and she hoped to keep at bay any further reaction. He gazed cautiously at her, and she used her best fake smile to reassure him that she was fine. She'd rehearsed and used that smile plenty of times for Charles, especially when he'd grown impatient with her illness if it interfered with his plans.

"Have you ever used anti-malarial drugs in place of cortico steroids?"

"I've tried every combination of treatment except chemotherapy."

Worry etched two lines between Jason's

brows, and in order to distract him she offered him a cluster of grapes, while she ate more cheese and bread, then took the extra pills. He sat next to her and patted her knee, nibbling on the grapes. At least he hadn't moved as far away as he could and acted as if she was a burden and spoiler of all things fun, as Charles often had.

"We'll take care of this," he said.

His earnest reassurance gave her hope he was a better man than her ex-husband.

As the clear sky darkened and the moon rose high and round above, Claire noticed mild aching in her muscles and joints, and hung her head in defeat. She feared this flare was beyond adding herbal remedies to her usual medicine, but she refused to give up and took more wild yam.

Jason watched her when she changed into her nightgown, and couldn't disguise his surprise at how quickly the rash had spread across her body, turning her bright pink.

"Oh, honey, what can I do for you?"

"I'll be OK, Jason. I'm just going to go to bed now and rest." It was only eight o'clock. She coughed as she turned back the covers.

"Let me listen to your lungs. Sometimes Lupus affects them."

She shook her head. "Not mine. Not so far, thanks to this special herb cocktail I take."

He reached for his doctor's bag in the storage bay on the opposite wall. "Indulge me. I'm worried about you."

She sat still while he placed the bell of his super-sized stethoscope on her back. He'd warmed it on his hand, yet still it felt cold against the heat of her rash and she straightened her spine. Her lungs were clear, as she knew they would be, but when Jason moved to her chest he listened intently.

"You have a murmur. Did you know that?"

"Mitral valve prolapse is a common problem with SLE. I've never had symptoms from it, though."

"No skipped beats or rapid pulse?"

"I only get that when I'm on heavy doses of

steroids. Or being ravished by you." That drew a smile from him.

"Let me put on some sunburn balm, at least." He put his stethoscope away and found some cool aloe gel. His hands were gentle and there was a caring look in his eyes as he applied it.

"I'm sorry to ruin your day," she said.

He stopped and shook his head. His ocean-gray eyes were clear with sincerity when he gazed into her face. "Other than your breaking out into a rash, this was the most perfect day I've had in years."

She brushed his lips with hers. "Thank you," she said, over his mouth.

They kissed again, and it was clear Jason wasn't sure how much pressure was OK to apply on her skin, or whether to touch her at all. After his hands grazed her arms but never settled, he solved his problem by digging his fingers into her sea-tossed hair and kissed her soundly.

He looked hungrily into her eyes. "I wish you were feeling better," he said.

"Me, too," she whispered.

With that, he tucked her into the bunk. "You warm that up for me later, OK?"

She smiled and nodded as she snuggled down into the pillow, hoping a good night's rest would solve her physical problems. As for her confusion over her growing feelings for Jason, that would take days to figure out.

"I'll be on the deck if you need anything," he said, shutting off the cabin light.

Claire closed her eyes and listened to his retreating footsteps. He'd called her "honey" and had said he thought he was falling for her, and it gave her hope that they could find a special meeting place. One that wasn't haunted by the past.

She'd wanted to make a good impression on the man she'd quickly come to care about. She hadn't set out to fall in love with Jason Rogers, but it seemed to be happening anyway. Why else would she strip buck naked and serve herself for lunch?

She covered her eyes and fought off a cringe, but soon remembered what had followed and decided she'd definitely done the right thing.

For the first time since her divorce, she wanted to be in a relationship again. If only her Lupus would cooperate.

Jason didn't deserve the burden of a chronically sick girlfriend. Not after all he'd been through. The thought made her queasy, though it could be the extra ibuprofen. Fighting off sleep, she lay and waited for him.

He couldn't bring himself to go to her. Sitting on the deck, listening to the waves lap his boat, Jason stared into the dark. A scattering of stars had already appeared, but the distant shore lights made them weak and dim. He'd slipped up earlier and said something that had shocked him. He wasn't ready to tell Claire how he really felt.

He thought about her below deck, stricken with a rash and Lupus flare, just because she'd spent the day on his sailboat. The last thing he wanted to do was cause her pain. One nagging morbid thought repeated itself. What if her disease progressed and one day he'd lose her? Could he allow himself to fall in love with another woman he might lose?

And, if that weren't enough to keep him awake all night, he still needed to work out his resistance to the little one. It wouldn't be fair to love Claire and not Gina, too. The child deserved nothing less.

But not from him. He wasn't her father.

"Hanna. Baby girl. I'd give anything to change places with you," he whispered into the dark.

He'd said it with conviction on so many occasions over the past four years that it took him awhile to recognize how hollow the words sounded this time. Had he said it out of habit, or did he still really want to die? He thought about Claire below in his bunk and longed to go to her but, burdened by a million thoughts, couldn't bring himself to move.

He was a doctor; he knew how to deal with illness, but…

Two children stood between them. One living. One dead.

Jason cupped his hands behind his head and stared intently into the blackening sky.

* * *

The next morning, though Claire's body aches and rash showed strong signs of improvement, they opted not to hike, and to sail home early.

By mid-morning, they approached the palm tree lined shore of Santa Barbara harbor, where Jason found his berth and docked.

"Before we pick up Gina," he said, "I'd like to drop off some of this gear."

Claire had never been to his house, and was interested in seeing where Jason lived. Twenty minutes later, just beyond the community college with the seaside track where a huge track and field meet was going on, they entered his Spanish-styled condo with arched entryway, red tiles and dark wood posts. The layout was open and inviting with the living room and dining room flowing into the surprisingly large kitchen complete with cooking island, and a terrace with an ocean view opening out from the dining area.

The first thing that hit her between the eyes was a large family portrait oil painting hanging on the living room wall. Seeing Jessica and

Hanna made her stop in her tracks. Jessica had large attractive eyes and full lips, and dark brown hair. She perched on the arm of the high-backed chair that Jason sat on with Hanna on his lap. A traditional pose. The little girl had thick, wavy hair down her shoulders, and bright inquisitive eyes. She was skinny and looked consumed by her father's large hands. The complete happiness evidenced in Jason's face was something she had yet to witness.

Her heart ached as she studied the portrait, and wondered if she could ever replace that joy. The thought made her shoulders slump.

Jason had bustled ahead down the hall to unload his gear. Rather than gawk at the portrait, and indulge her worst fears, Claire glanced around the room. The long tastefully upholstered couch had most likely been chosen by Jessica. The lamps looked like Tiffany heirlooms. On a nearby table was a box of shoes by a brand Claire particularly liked but could never afford. She lifted the lid, expecting to find a pair of stylish stiletto pumps, perhaps Jessica's, but found a pair of bronzed booties with Hanna's birth date inscribed in the stand; a well chewed combination teething ring and baby rattle made out of silver; a slab of clay, brightly painted and glazed, with Hanna's hand print on it; a homemade Father's Day card from the year of the accident; a mother's locket with Hanna's picture inside; a multi-jeweled necklace and matching earrings fit for a rich doctor's wife; a half empty bottle of perfume, a brand far too expensive for Claire to ever consider buying; a Valentine's card for Jason from Jessica, which Claire did not open; and a mangled wedding ring. A platinum cushion-cut diamond rock that had lost several of the smaller stones outlining the warped band.

Claire's pulse sped up when she realized the ring would have had to be removed from Jessica's hand after the accident. Her heart ached for Jason. Tears welled up in her eyes as she realized the significance of this box, and she bit her lip to keep from crying.

Jason found her there, holding the ring.

"I'm sorry," she said, swiping at her lashes. "I didn't mean to snoop. I expected to find a pair of shoes, not this."

Jason picked up the box and reached for the ring. "That's how we finally identified her." He studied the misshapen object. "They had to use metal cutters to get it off her finger." With a distant look in his eyes, he put it back in the box and closed the lid.

At least now, Claire knew where he kept his heart.

CHAPTER NINE

"CAN we talk about this?" Claire asked, gesturing toward the box.

Last night on the deck, Jason had thought long and hard about their situation. His family. Claire's Lupus. Her daughter. His daughter. The time they shared with each other, and his losses, which could never be recovered. He wanted Claire, though he didn't know where a relationship with her might lead since he still didn't know if he could separate Hanna from Gina.

He needed to delay what he suspected Claire wanted to discuss. He glanced toward the kitchen. "I'll make some lunch," he said.

"I don't think I could eat," Claire replied, an earnest appeal in her eyes.

She'd found the shoe box. Clearly, she wanted to talk about his family and letting go. The last thing he felt ready for. His stomach clenched as he led her out to the terrace and gestured for her to sit in the shaded area. "At least let me get you some water or soda."

"Let's just talk," she said, patting the chair next to her.

He sat, but couldn't get comfortable, leaned forward, edgy, and tried not to jiggle his foot.

"Now that I've gotten to know the other side of you, Jason, I'd like to have a relationship with you. It's scary for me to admit, because my ex-husband made me feel like I'm not much of a catch."

"He's an ass," he said. Anything to avoid what he feared would come next. "No disrespect to Gina's daddy, but the guy did a terrible thing to you."

"I'm glad you feel that way." She sighed. "You know me. I like to lay my cards on the table." She glanced at him with a nervous flutter of lashes. "Jason, you've come so far, you've opened up and shown me another side of you I never dreamed existed. You're a decent and honorable man, and I love that about you. You've shared your passion for sailing—" she blushed and her voice lowered "—and for making love with me."

He liked that even after they'd been together several times, and she'd stripped buck naked for him, she could still turn pink and look uneasy discussing their sex life. But he'd as near as told her he loved her, and she hadn't come close to repeating the sentiments. The topic was a touchy one, to say the least, and his silence wasn't making it any easier for her. Every muscle in his body tensed rather than blurt out the truth. He loved her, but didn't think he'd ever make it over the hurdle where Gina was concerned.

"I…uh…heard what you said yesterday in the galley," she said. "I wanted to say something back, but…uh…you made me very distracted." She forced a nervous smile, making her lip twitch at the corner. "But it's been four years, and a huge part of your life is still in that box."

Rather than look at him, she gazed off in the

distance at the ocean. He wondered if it was because she was afraid what she'd see in his eyes, or what he'd see in hers. He wanted to grab her hands and tell her not to worry. To give him more time. He felt confident he could work through this if she'd just give him a little more time.

But the best he could promise was maybe. Would that be enough for her?

"I don't expect you to ever forget Jessica or Hanna. Please don't get me wrong, I don't want to replace anything. I just want a shot at getting all of you, not the leftovers." Her gaze settled on him, and he sat perfectly still, knowing how hard it must be for her to tell him this. "I guess what I'm doing is laying myself on the line."

He understood what she was getting at, but felt pushed in a direction he wasn't completely ready to go. "You mean like giving me an ultimatum? Move on or else?" The spoken words sounded harsher than when he'd thought them.

She looked quickly at him, as if startled by his blunt assessment.

"Look, I know I've been holding out on you, Claire. I'm trying to change. I thought we had a pretty damn great weekend."

Her smile was weak. "We did."

"It's just that I've been in this holding pattern so long, I'm stuck." He leaned forward, resting his elbows on his knees, earnestly searching her eyes. "I want a relationship with you, too." He reached for her hand. "I have feelings for you, please know that."

She squeezed his knuckles. "And I have feelings for you, too, but I don't know how we can explore them if…" She glanced at the shoe box.

If I don't let go of my dead family? "I know what you're saying. And I'm not going to revert to my mantra about how you can't possibly understand how hard it is to lose what I've lost."

"No one could ever know that, and I'm not trying to make less of it. My heart aches for you and your losses. I can only imagine the pain you've gone through, and it makes sense to want to protect yourself from more pain. But Jason, it's time to make a decision whether you want to continue living half a life alone in a carefully protected world, or risk living a full life with someone else but with the possibility of more pain."

The ongoing doubt forced a new wave of frustration through his chest. He dug his fingers in his hair and exhaled. "Don't you think I know that? I've thought about it every single day since I met you."

She nodded. "There's no way we can know the future. We may wind up just having an affair and hating each other." With a half-hearted smile she swung her arm dramatically, as if trying to lighten the mood. "Who knows?"

"I can't believe that." He smiled and patted her knee. "It's more than just sex with us."

A quiet laugh escaped her lips. "I don't know, the sex is pretty good." She shook her head and quickly grew serious again.

"Since we've gotten to know each other I've been beating myself up over my stubborn ways. It's just that I've been living like this for so long, I..."

"Maybe your stubborn attitude is telling you something. Maybe it's my Lupus?"

"No! I know we can deal with that. I want to keep you healthy and, between your medical knowledge and mine, there's no reason we can't do that." He'd be damned if he'd brand her as damaged and unworthy of love like her ex-husband had.

"I can't even go sailing with you without breaking into a rash," she said.

He lifted a skeptical brow. That was the least of his worries about pursuing a relationship with Claire. "Haven't you ever heard of sunset cruising? And besides, if I'd been more attentive and kept you out of the sun, this may never have happened."

The corners of her mouth twisted up into a cautious smile, but it didn't reach her eyes. She laced her fingers together and stared at her hands. "Then maybe it's Gina?"

Oh, damn, he didn't want to talk about this.

What kind of jerk had second thoughts about a woman's child? He glanced towards the shoe box, thinking of Hanna's tiny handprint.

Claire saw a telling glint in Jason's eyes. He'd hesitated when she'd asked the most pressing question written in her heart, and he seemed incapable of giving her a straight answer. She'd been afraid to ask it, but after he hadn't slept with her last night, she knew something was wrong and needed to know the answer, no matter how painful it might be. He'd said it wasn't her Lupus and, barring any other unforeseen problems, that left her daughter.

She swallowed her disappointment, and took his hands in hers. "All we can do is see where things go. I'm not asking you to forget your family. I'm just asking you to quit living in that box." She needed to be more direct, to let him know things couldn't go on if he had any doubt about accepting her daughter. "And one more thing, Jason. I'm a package deal. If you can't…"

Her cellphone rang. Their eyes met for a

moment-of-truth stare. She saw a flicker of fear before he blinked.

After a brief conversation with her ex-husband, filled with excuses and a change of plans, she hung up. Charles had been the biggest disappointment in her life, but Jason was on the verge of breaking her heart. She swallowed back the bitter taste of defeat, and decided to revert to business as usual.

"That was Charles. Good thing we got home early today, because he wants to drop off Gina already." The irony curved her mouth into a sarcastic smile. "He's probably tired of entertaining her. He doesn't understand that kids are perfectly capable of keeping themselves busy. All she wants is to know someone who loves her is around."

Jason rose, not uttering a sound. He headed to the door to give Claire a ride home. As they walked to the car, he thought about Gina, and Claire's comment about how all Gina wanted was to know someone who loved her was around. He had that in common with the little one. On impulse, he hooked his arm through Claire's, swung her around and kissed her. "Don't give up on me."

She didn't answer, and he couldn't discern what was written in her eyes.

Half an hour later, after a long and silent drive, they arrived at Claire's home. A tall thin man with pale, deep-set eyes and longish brown hair paced back and forth. Gina swung happily on the makeshift rope and wood contraption Mrs. Densmore had managed to hang from the ancient oak tree on the property when they'd first moved in. She wore purple denim overalls, with a big pocket on her chest.

"Puth me, Daddy! Wee, look at meeeee. Mommy!"

Gina almost jumped from the swing when she saw them, and Claire sprinted to her side before she could fall on her hands and knees in the gravel or, worse yet, her face. She exhaled an exasperated sigh and flashed an irritated glance toward Charles, who hadn't been nearly close enough to protect Gina.

"Listen, I've got to go. Willow has tickets to the Starlight bowl tonight, and she wants to meet up with some friends for dinner first," Charles said.

"Thanks for watching her."

"No problem," he said, brushing a kiss across Gina's cheek. "Bye, tweety-bird"

"You tweety-burd," Gina said with a giggle, swatting at his face.

When Charles drove off, big drops of tears fell from Gina's eyes, and Claire scooped her into her arms and hugged her tight. "I missed you so much," she said.

Gina rested her head on Claire's shoulder. "Mommy," she sighed, as if she were finally home.

Jason glimpsed a moment that perfectly explained how he'd felt about Claire since last weekend. Not that she was a mommy figure, but that she felt like home. A new and exciting place he'd forgotten existed. She was steadfast and understanding, and she'd never let anyone down if she could help it, especially someone she loved. And she'd made her point perfectly clear. *Take both of us or nothing at all.*

He wanted a new start. With her.

He loved her. He did. He loved her.

After the dizzying revelation, instead of running off, he wanted nothing more than to stay with her. "Mind if I come in for a while?"

"I'd like that," Claire said.

With her father gone, Gina discovered Jason's presence, and squealed, "Dock-to Wah-durs!"

"Hey, squirt, you glad to see me?"

Claire let her down and she ran toward Jason. She took his hand and started chatting away while leading him into the house. "I had wunch at MicDonauds..."

Jason had hoped to pick up the conversation with Claire where they'd left off, to bargain for more time in her good graces, but Gina had other plans. She walked him down the hall to her room and grabbed her favorite book.

"Read me."

He started the story about a corduroy bear, and glanced down at her curls. They looked soft, and a tender feeling whispered through him. He read to distract himself from the feelings.

Claire took her overnight case to her room, and when she'd unpacked she stopped by long enough to say she was going to check up on Mrs. Densmore.

After fifteen more minutes of Gina handing him book after book, Claire reappeared at the door. "Gina, honey, I need to talk to Dr. Rogers."

"He read me." He'd just finished reading a book about a princess marrying a prince, and she handed him yet another one, after she picked up a doll half as big as her.

"Maybe later," Claire said.

"Read." Gina ignored her mother and opened the book for Jason, then pointed to the page where she wanted him to start.

Claire crossed the room, removed the book from Jason's hands and gave the girl a stern stare. "No. That's enough for now."

Gina screwed up her face and threw her dolly

down. She opened her mouth without making a peep while tears pooled in her eyes. After what seemed like several seconds, a long wrenching wail finally escaped her mouth.

Claire dropped to her knees and cupped the little girl's arms. "Calm down, Gina. Get a hold of yourself."

Uncharacteristically, Gina swung at her mother and stomped her foot. "No!" she said. "No!"

"Sometimes she gets like this after being with her father," Claire said over her shoulder, a pleading look in her eye. "I'm not sure if it's because he spoils her, or if it's just too hard for her to say goodbye." Claire held her daughter close, though she squirmed and flung her head around. "What's wrong, Gina? Use your words."

"No!"

"If you can't calm down, I'm going to put you on time out to help you."

"No!"

Remaining calm, Claire stood up and took

Gina by the hand, picked up one of her kiddy-sized chairs and led her to the end of the hall. "Sit," she said, matter of factly.

To Jason's amazement, Gina sat facing the wall, fussing and sobbing. The kid knew the routine.

"Two minutes," Claire said, without a hint of emotion in her voice.

Gina grumbled and kicked the wall she faced.

"I'm not setting the clock until you quiet down."

More grumbling. Jason tried not to crack a smile.

Claire sighed and rolled her eyes as she tiptoed down the hall, bringing Jason along with her to the kitchen, where she set an egg timer. "Sorry about that."

"Hey, I've seen this behavior plenty of times. It's got to be hard on her, going back and forth between two parents."

Claire nodded. "In a perfect world, right?"

He knew exactly what she was talking about.

"Can I make you some coffee?"

Happy to be invited to stick around, he nodded. "Sounds good." He listened for a moment. "Hey, the squirt has quieted down."

"Works every time. Thank God for time outs." Claire flashed a brilliant smile, and Jason couldn't stop himself from kissing her. Just when their lips were getting warmed up, the egg timer went off.

Claire broke away. "Time's up, Gina," she called out. She strode toward the kitchen door, peeked outside, then sprinted down the hall.

A scream rent the air and Jason rushed to find Claire holding a limp Gina in her arms.

"What's wrong?" he said.

"I don't know if she's having an allergic reaction to something or choking."

Gina's face was blotchy and pink, her eyes dilated wide. She didn't appear to be breathing. "Gina said they'd eaten at McDonald's. Is she allergic to any food?"

"Nothing that I know of."

Jason grabbed Gina from Claire as an epiphany hit him between the eyes. He couldn't save his own daughter, but by God he wouldn't allow this child to die!

"Call 911," he said as he rushed her down the hall to the better lighting in the living room. Gina wasn't breathing. He opened her mouth to try to see if there was anything blocking her windpipe. He thought he glimpsed something, but knew he could make things worse by trying to pull it out.

As Claire paced and talked on the phone, giving all the specific information, Jason turned Gina over his arm and gave her five strong strikes between her shoulders, then flipped her over to check her mouth again. He thought the object was a little more evident, but Gina still was unable to breathe. Her lips were turning blue and her little fingers had gone limp. Her eyes were fluttering open and closed. He laid her head-down on his thigh and used the cuff of his hand to push upward five times on her sternum. There was no response, so he repeated the procedure of slapping her back and pushing on her diaphragm several more times. He'd lost count, but knew he was working against the clock. Gina hadn't gotten oxygen for at least two minutes. He worried what the consequences would be.

With the cuff of his hand pushing upward above her stomach, he heard something pop. He looked inside the mouth of the lifeless child and found a tiny plastic figure.

"Your fingers are smaller than mine," he said to Claire. "Can you dislodge that?"

Claire was on the job in a heartbeat and pulled out a tiny toy from her daughter's throat. Then discovered a couple more inside her bib pocket. Had they come from the lunchbox toy?

Gina had been unconscious long enough to not automatically start breathing on her own. Jason knew choking was the number one cause of cardiac arrest in children. He felt for a brachial pulse, and thankfully found one, then he gave two quick puffs of air into her mouth.

Gina coughed and spluttered, and soon the sweetest sound emitted from her lungs—she cried. Loudly. Music to his ears.

He glanced at Claire, holding Gina as the firemen and emergency techs stormed the house. Claire explained everything that had happened, all the way back to where Gina had had lunch.

"That's exactly why the packages say ages three and up," one of the firemen said.

"He saved her life." She pointed at Jason and smiled with tears shimmering in her eyes. He saw love and admiration there. When he glanced at Gina, as the emergency personnel worked on her, he took a deep breath and suddenly knew everything would be all right.

In the height of the emergency one clear thought had come to him—he loved Gina just as much as he loved Claire. He loved them both. They were the most important people in his life. And life could be taken away in an instant. If he waited for the assurance that he'd never lose a loved one again, he'd die a lonely man.

If it came down to protecting himself and being alone, or letting his heart continue to come alive, even if it meant feeling the dagger of loss, he was finally willing to take the risk.

He rushed to Claire and took her into his arms as they rolled Gina out the door.

"The mother can come along," one of the men said.

Claire grabbed her purse and ran alongside the gurney.

"I'll meet you there," Jason called out.

"I'm counting on it," she said with a wave just before climbing into the back of the ambulance.

He'd finally let himself be counted on again, and that sealed the last gap in his heart.

CHAPTER TEN

THREE hours later, Gina had been admitted to the hospital for overnight observation. The ordeal had worn her out. She napped peacefully in the crib-sized bed in the Peds unit, and Claire couldn't take her eyes off her. Soft brown curls haloed her head, thick dark lashes kissed her cheeks, and her Cupid's bow lips puckered and twitched from time to time.

Jason sat quietly across the room in one of the two chairs. He'd been by her side through every horrific moment of the choking ordeal.

"In one instant I felt the magnitude of your losses, Jason." Claire looked at him with the recollection of every ounce of pain she had felt so heavily in her heart. "I'm amazed you were ever able to function at all."

He laughed ruefully. “I think you figured out soon enough I wasn’t.”

Claire was torn between running to Jason and hugging him and leaving her baby’s bedside. She wasn’t ready to let go of Gina’s dimpled fingers. The child slept quietly, eyes moving behind her lids. What dreams she must be having, Claire thought. She’d been fighting off a headache since finding Gina unconscious. The memory made her heart speed up again.

Jason appeared beside her, as if reading her body language, and put his hand on her shoulder. “It took almost losing our Gina to get me to see the light,” he said.

Our Gina. Claire liked the sound of that phrase. She sighed and rested her head on his shoulder. “And what light was that?”

“Life is too short to drag my feet. I’m not going to waste another moment of it.” He turned Claire to face him and studied her eyes. “I was lying when I said I was falling for you.”

She tensed and mini-fireworks shot off in her chest. Did he actually want to back-pedal with her at Gina’s bedside? Had she completely misread the whole weekend and their earlier conversation?

"I'd already fallen in love. I started feeling it the day I saw you dancing with that bee, and I've continued to feel it grow, step by step, each day you've graced my life."

After her heart did a quick spin, she broke into a smile and threw her arms around his neck in relief. He caressed her, but continued talking.

"What I'm trying to say is I want the three of us to be a family. I love you, and I want to marry you. I've waited long enough to breathe again."

Thoughts spun through Claire's head. She'd been coming to a similar conclusion about Jason. Day by day he'd passed her office door and, against his will, he'd turned and wished her a good morning. He'd begrudgingly followed his innate will to live and had gotten involved with her. And it had taken another near tragedy to bring him to his senses.

"I've never jumped into anything so fast in my life," he said. "But I've lost a hell of a lot of time and I don't want to waste another moment."

He covered her mouth with warm lips and reminded her of the special chemistry they shared. How often in life did a person get such an opportunity to be with someone so perfect for them?

The strangest thing was, now that he'd laid it on the line for her, as she'd done at his house earlier that afternoon, she was the one with reservation in her heart. Could she trust him?

They kissed again.

He was the most trustworthy man she'd ever met.

His fingers splayed at the back of her head and moved her closer to deepen the bedside kiss.

Would he stick by her side when she had relapses? He'd told her as much earlier. He'd already nursed her back to health a couple of times, and who better to care for her Lupus than a man who understood the disease? He was a doctor, and he'd be entering the marriage with his eyes wide open.

His tongue traced the lining of her mouth.

She'd worried that he couldn't accept Gina, but hadn't he fought for her life like a true hero?

The way a father would fight for his child? She'd be forever grateful to him for saving her. She didn't need him to prove himself, but seeing him desperately working to keep her daughter alive had completed her love for him.

Claire pressed her tongue to his and gave him one last kiss. She pulled back so she could look into his eyes. Jason was a man who had never wanted to love again, yet he was also a man who had proved himself to her in a thousand little ways over the last couple of months.

She glanced at her daughter, who still seemed to be sleeping.

If Jason could make this huge leap of faith in love, why couldn't she?

"I see a million thoughts swimming behind those eyes, Claire. We can have as long an engagement as you want; if that will help you make up your mind."

"Oh, Jason, this is all so sudden."

"I just want to know one thing. Whether it's today or next week or next year, do you love me?"

"I do, Jason. I love you with all my heart."

"Then will you marry me?"

"Marry you? Oh, Jason, this is the craziest day of my life."

A creaking on the crib springs drew their attention to Gina, who'd sat up.

"Thay yeth, Mommy."

Claire and Jason laughed together when they found Gina's precocious blue eyes wide and alert, and a smile tickled across her mouth. "Thay yeth."

And suddenly Claire thought with all of her heart that it was a great idea.

One month later

Claire left René Munroe's exam room a bit in a daze. She fidgeted with her engagement ring as she took the stairs toward her office. She'd been mildly queasy over the weekend when they'd taken the sailboat out, but had blamed it on the choppy sea.

The first clue had been yesterday when, for the first time in her life, she'd become a sympathy puker. One of her patients had come in complaining of a gall bladder attack, and when the cholecystitis had caused the patient to use an emesis basin, Claire had needed one too.

This morning when she'd woken up with a familiar feeling, and opted for saltine crackers for breakfast instead of her usual oatmeal, she'd asked René to examine her.

She approached Jason's office full of jitters.

"Hi, honey. What's up?" he said.

She loved how his eyes always brightened when he saw her, and how, since they'd been engaged, she'd never once doubted his true feelings for her.

"You know how you left it up to me to put the time limit on our engagement?" she said.

"Yep."

"I'm calling it in."

He cocked his head and narrowed one eye. "Why the sudden change?"

"I'm pregnant."

He hopped from behind his desk to hug her. "This is great news!"

She told him the due date René had just given

her and, instead of being worried, she laughed. She was engaged to a wonderful guy and she wouldn't trade one day of their romance… except maybe for that first day at MidCoast Medical clinic. Nah. Not even that!

Just that morning they'd had a minor clash over what he still referred to as her *woo woo* alternative medicine. He wasn't sure about her suggestion of acupuncture for one of the patients who'd had little success with traditional smoking cessation techniques. But he'd come around and had agreed to give it a try.

And as Charles had seemed to fade into the background where Gina was concerned, Jason had gladly stepped forward. And Gina had rewarded him with a new name—Daddy Wahdurs.

Little did she know…

Jason kissed Claire and together they did the math right back to the first night when they'd been together. His gaze fused with hers and a tender smile lifted one corner of his mouth. "I guess some things are just meant to be."

MEDICAL™

Large Print

Titles for the next six months...

October

THE NURSE'S BROODING BOSS	Laura Iding
EMERGENCY DOCTOR AND CINDERELLA	Melanie Milburne
CITY SURGEON, SMALL TOWN MIRACLE	Marion Lennox
BACHELOR DAD, GIRL NEXT DOOR	Sharon Archer
A BABY FOR THE FLYING DOCTOR	Lucy Clark
NURSE, NANNY...BRIDE!	Alison Roberts

November

THE SURGEON'S MIRACLE	Caroline Anderson
DR DI ANGELO'S BABY BOMBSHELL	Janice Lynn
NEWBORN NEEDS A DAD	Dianne Drake
HIS MOTHERLESS LITTLE TWINS	Dianne Drake
WEDDING BELLS FOR THE VILLAGE NURSE	Abigail Gordon
HER LONG-LOST HUSBAND	Josie Metcalfe

December

THE MIDWIFE AND THE MILLIONAIRE	Fiona McArthur
FROM SINGLE MUM TO LADY	Judy Campbell
KNIGHT ON THE CHILDREN'S WARD	Carol Marinelli
CHILDREN'S DOCTOR, SHY NURSE	Molly Evans
HAWAIIAN SUNSET, DREAM PROPOSAL	Joanna Neil
RESCUED: MOTHER AND BABY	Anne Fraser

MEDICAL™

Large Print

January

DARE SHE DATE THE DREAMY DOC?	Sarah Morgan
DR DROP-DEAD GORGEOUS	Emily Forbes
HER BROODING ITALIAN SURGEON	Fiona Lowe
A FATHER FOR BABY ROSE	Margaret Barker
NEUROSURGEON…AND MUM!	Kate Hardy
WEDDING IN DARLING DOWNS	Leah Martyn

February

WISHING FOR A MIRACLE	Alison Roberts
THE MARRY-ME WISH	Alison Roberts
PRINCE CHARMING OF HARLEY STREET	Anne Fraser
THE HEART DOCTOR AND THE BABY	Lynne Marshall
THE SECRET DOCTOR	Joanna Neil
THE DOCTOR'S DOUBLE TROUBLE	Lucy Clark

March

DATING THE MILLIONAIRE DOCTOR	Marion Lennox
ALESSANDRO AND THE CHEERY NANNY	Amy Andrews
VALENTINO'S PREGNANCY BOMBSHELL	Amy Andrews
A KNIGHT FOR NURSE HART	Laura Iding
A NURSE TO TAME THE PLAYBOY	Maggie Kingsley
VILLAGE MIDWIFE, BLUSHING BRIDE	Gill Sanderson